I0601987

BITTER
VOWS

CRIMSON FALLS DUET BOOK ONE

DANI RENÉ

Cover Design: Jay Aheer, Simply Defined Art
Cover Photography: Regina Wamba
Editing: Candice Royer
Proofing: Illuminate Author Services

DEDICATION

To the girls who prefer the Big Bad Wolf because he's an expert when it comes to eating you.

PLAYLIST

Desire - Meg Myers
Beggin For Thread - BANKS
Fuck Em Only We Know - BANKS
Man or a Monster - Sam Tinnesz, Zayde Wølf
Pretty Head - Transviolet
Like You - EXES
Find You - Ruelle
I Know Your Secrets - Tommee Profitt, Fleurie, Jung Youth
If I Want To - Usher
Lonely Together - Sofia Karlberg

If you'd like to listen to the rest of songs that inspired this story, the playlist is on Spotify.

DEDICATION

To the girls who prefer the Big Bad Wolf
because he's an expert when it comes to
eating you.

PLAYLIST

Desire - Meg Myers

Beggin For Thread - BANKS

Fuck Em Only We Know - BANKS

Man or a Monster - Sam Tinnesz, Zayde Wølf

Pretty Head - Transviolet

Like You - EXES

Find You - Ruelle

I Know Your Secrets - Tommee Profitt, Fleurie, Jung Youth

If I Want To - Usher

Lonely Together - Sofia Karlberg

If you'd like to listen to the rest of songs that inspired this story, the playlist is on Spotify.

LYCAN

Life doesn't afford us many chances to make right what we've done wrong.

It also doesn't allow us to apologize to those who have passed—no longer walking this earth. When I was younger, the guilt ate away at me. Inch by inch, my soul was consumed by the incessant culpability taking hold of me, but then I realized— if I allow myself to *feel*, I'll never survive. Instead of allowing sentiment to burrow its way inside me, I've buried what most would call *human emotions*. And all I'm left with is the ice-cold ruthlessness that grips me.

Especially growing up with the family I did. The Shaw name was synonymous with violence and bloodshed, and even though I should walk

1

away, change it, I don't. I'm proud of the fact that we're known as people you do not cross. My brother decided to walk away from it all. It hurt at first, but now, I realize family isn't always blood.

Choices are what guide us, taking us through the darkness that's been holding us hostage for so long that when we look up into the light, we don't recognize it. Over the years, I've become accustomed to the shadows, and I've basked in them. I no longer want an escape.

Strolling through my club, Heaven, I stop when I reach the immaculate mahogany bar. I cast a glance over the large, dimly lit space, taking in each patron who has already entered my domain. When I opened this place, it was meant for those who wanted to play, to indulge in fantasies that aren't *normal*, and even though my tastes are eclectic, I didn't realize just how dark some tendencies go. I've learned, though, and I've reveled in the shadows.

Black suede booths curl around silver-legged tables, which seats four people. Each one private as they snake against the far wall. To the left of the bar is the entrance to the club, which is where we've just come from, and I notice how it's hidden by the sleek, black, silken curtains that keep this space private.

Stools line the bar area, and to the right is the hallway, which leads to rooms where the games begin. Once the couples or groups have acquainted themselves and agreed to an evening's festivities, they move to one of the private rooms.

Some like to be watched, so I've ensured that there is space for them as well. Every person who walks into Heaven finds solace, pleasure, and satisfaction. When they leave, it's as if all that happened within these walls are a memory, a happy one, but nothing more than an escape from their harsh reality.

I take in the customers who are settled with drinks. The men in expensive, tailored suits and the beautiful women draped over their arms—eye candy. Most of the politicians and businessmen who frequent Heaven are corrupt, married, or owned by the mafia.

My club offers them a cover for the activities which Heaven is famed for. With Masters and slaves, Dominants and their submissives, along with single women who crave the degradation and humiliation that's usually frowned upon, I've given them somewhere to enjoy their desires.

But everything comes with a price.

Everything.

Membership is not cheap, but there are rules that govern every person who walks in the door, and even after they leave, they know that confidentiality is key. Isaac, the barman who's worked for me for years, slides over a tumbler with deep amber liquid.

"Thanks."

"Busy night?" he asks, knowing that I'll have the headcount before the doors open. I only allow so many people in the club at a time, and each night, I limit the number of patrons who enter Heaven.

"Yes, we have a special party tonight," I tell him before I take a sip of my drink, watching the couples slowly forming as they get to know each other. Each woman who walks in here has signed an agreement that she understands what happens in here stays here. And each man knows that he will immediately cease all play if he is told to stop.

My cell phone buzzes in my pocket, and when I pull it out, I notice a familiar name—Alexei Carnevali. One of the Mafia princes I've known since I was a kid. We grew up together, did shit while studying at university, and now that we each have our own companies, we've become closer than I anticipated.

"Alex," I greet after pressing the phone to my ear. "To what do I owe this honor?"

"I was wondering if you can help me," he starts. "I have a job coming up which I'm certain would interest you." I can hear the excitement in his tone, and I have to admit, my interest is piqued.

"Oh? I'm always open to working with you. Especially if it means bloodshed." I signal for another drink as he chuckles at my response, my gaze landing on the door as two patrons saunter in. One is an influential politician, the other, someone I've been keeping my eye on. His money has been his downfall, and his wife has no fucking clue about his proclivities.

"There's a convent about two hours outside of Los Angeles, which I need your men to check up on, and since you have connections over there, I figured you'd be the best person to ask. I've heard rumors of the Cartel moving illegal goods into the States, trading them up from the border to the City of Angels."

My ears perk up at his words. "Illegal goods?" I've had connections all over the country, all over the world, but if Alex is coming to me, then this must be big. Even though he must have people down there, I have a feeling this goes deeper than just the Cartel.

"Girls." The one word has me on my feet. My target for the evening is moving toward the booths, a woman on his arm that isn't his wife, and even though my blood is boiling with the need to take him down, what Alex just confessed is more important.

"Send me the info. I'll have them shut down within a few hours. Blood will spill."

"If I were closer, I would ask you to wait for me, but I'm in Italy; a job that needed my attention," he informs me. The lowering of his tone tells me he's not alone.

If he's in Europe, then I wonder where his *familia* is. "What about your cousins?" I know the Moretti brothers are based in LA. I've never met them personally, but I've spent enough time with Alex to know they're not men you mess around with.

"They're... indisposed. Miami needed their attention." His voice tinged with mystery has me pondering what they're up to, but I know better than to ask. I don't get into their business, and they don't get into mine.

Nodding to myself, I tell him, "I'll sort this out." The promise is there as I move into my spacious office, drink in one hand, my phone in the other. Kicking the door shut behind me, I settle behind my cherry wood desk. The sleek leather chair molds to my form, and I relax against it before waking my computer with a nudge to the mouse. When the screen lights up, Alex's encrypted email is waiting. "I've got the info; just leave it with me. I'll confirm once the job is done."

"Talk soon." He hangs up before I can say anything more, but there's nothing else I can tell him. I hit dial on Kahn's number. The one man I know will have a vested interest in this.

It takes him two rings before answering. "Mr. Shaw."

"Kahn, I have a job for you and the team. I know

6

you're out on the East Coast right now, but before you dive into training, I'd like you to check out a convent," I tell him, leaning back in my chair, casting my gaze down at the club below.

Silence greets me for a long moment before he responds, "A convent?"

"Alexei Carnevali just called," I inform my best man. "He has it on good authority that illegal goods are being moved from New York to Mexico. The Cartel is involved, but we can't walk into their territory without proof, or we will start a war."

"Goods? As in…?" He allows his words to filter into the silence between us, and each time I think about what Alex told me, the more my blood boils at the thought of what's happening to innocent women.

"Yes."

"I'm on it," Kahn tells me, raw honesty in his tone, but also a hint of the hunter I know him to be. That's why I hired him when he first walked into my club. A man with the desire of a predator and the skill of a trained assassin. *What more could I want?*

"Good. Keep me updated." I hang up, my glare still on the thieving asshole downstairs. Mr. Bardot is nothing more than a cheating scumbag, but he doesn't realize just how he's about to pay me back for walking in when I had to.

A fucking Bardot coming in and ruining shit in

my life once more. It's not the first time I've had to learn about their family. The name is synonymous with secrets. The Bardot family come from old money, and with the help of his mother, Grace Bardot, they stole more from us than just a few million.

But then I learned more about Horatio. He's got problems, some than money won't fix. I only found out because I looked into why he spent far too much time in my club. It was then I realized something was amiss.

At first, I thought it was my good for nothing brother, but Darius had no access to funds, not mine anyway. Not Shaw money. But there's more to the story than just the money. The problem is that Horatio has lost a lot more than his livelihood. He's about to lose something far more precious to him.

With a sardonic grin on my face, I push to my feet, button my suit jacket, and make my way down to the main area of the club. Time to speak to Mr. Bardot and ensure that his signature is on the contract before he even thinks of playing in one of my rooms tonight.

Only, he doesn't know just how expensive his *needs* have become.

SCARLETT

The sleek, silver dress that drapes over my curves is beautiful, but even as I stare at myself in the mirror, I'm torn between going to this party or staying home. My mother, Marinda Bardot, is one of the most publicized socialites, while my father, Horatio Bardot, is working hard to get into the senator's office.

Wealth comes at a steep price, and they don't realize it. Since I was a child, I knew what I wanted to do, and it wasn't to be the pretty arm candy my mother would like me to be. I have goals, dreams, and they don't involve a man putting a diamond on my finger and knocking me up while he goes to his pristine office to run a Fortune 500 company.

I want to be the CEO of my own life, but with the

Bardot name comes responsibility I'm not ready for. Granted, my gran, who I look up to, will understand if I told her my plans. Because of her, I was able to get an internship in New York in a few months.

My folks were not happy about that, but they acquiesced because Gran wanted it. Slipping my feet into the four-inch heeled sandals, I take in my outfit, my long, red hair plaited in a thick braid down to the middle of my back. Stray curls have already come loose, but I don't tie them back. My wide, dark eyes are lined with black, my lashes darkened by mascara, and my lips are shimmering from the gloss painted over the deep red lipstick.

Perfectly poised.

I silently make my way out to the hallway, listening for my parents arguing, but find silence. Thankfully, they haven't already started fighting, but the night is still young. By the time I reach the foyer, my mother appears from the dining room, a flute of champagne already in hand, her eyes sparkling as she takes me in.

"Oh, Scarlett," she coos. "You look beautiful. There'll be so many men wanting to dance with you this evening. I hope you're ready." Her excitement about finding me a man makes me want to run back upstairs and hide in my room. At my age, I should've moved out of the house already, but I stayed. Mainly to keep an eye on my folks, but also, I've always felt safe in my childhood home.

"Well, they'll have to form a line," I tell her with a fake smile plastered on my lips. If there's one thing she's taught me to do well, that's pretending. It's not that I wouldn't like to be with someone, but the fact that she wants to marry me off to the most eligible bachelor leaves a bad taste in my mouth.

Laughter bounces from her lips, sounding like a tinkling coin against the expensive tiles as my father saunters toward us, a tight smile on his face and a gaze that flickers with apprehension. I notice the tension taut in his shoulders as he takes us in. "Are you ready?" he asks, his focus on me, and I nod. It doesn't take my mother long to swallow down her drink, and soon enough, we're in the town car as it weaves down our long driveway.

My phone buzzes in my purse, and I find a message from my best friend, Aelin. The moment I walked into class and settled beside her, I knew I'd found a connection. She looked over at me, her silver eyes shimmering as she took me in. Her smile was genuine, nothing like girls and women from the social circles I've been used to growing up. It was refreshing.

"I hope you're not going to sit on your phone all night, Scarlett," my mother admonishes, which I was expecting. The fact that I do have friends outside the people she knows doesn't sit well with my mother. It never has.

"Leave the girl, Marinda," Dad tells her, his gaze meeting hers. Something passes between them unspoken, which has ice trickling down my spine. My father turns his attention on me, offering me a smile that doesn't reach his eyes. He's never lied to me. I know this because when Dad would tell me something serious, he would always meet my gaze, but his next words are uttered with his stare on the seat behind me. "It's nice that you have friends. Your future might change in an instant, and who knows when you'll need someone to talk to."

"What do you mean?" There's a twisting in my gut, a coiling serpent tightening with every silent second that passes. My father's expression is one of guilt when he looks to my mother, then me.

"Just that Aelin is a nice girl. You should keep in contact with her." He waves his hand as if dismissing the topic, and I know if I ask anything more, he'll only ignore me. When my father decides to keep things to himself, there's no way of getting him to open up.

I don't respond, merely nod and continue with my reply to Aelin, letting her know I'm on my way and I'll see her soon. The charity ball is being held in town in a lavish, five-star hotel with only celebrities and politicians in attendance. The guestlist is filled with names that most would be excited to rub shoulders with, including Aelin's dad, who's one of the most well-known names across the world, a famous rock star with a penchant for causing women to drop to their knees. And soon, my best friend will be on tour with the band, leaving me to a lonely summer with my grandmother in Crimson Falls.

Thankfully, I enjoy spending time at the manor house, or I would be depressed having to spend time at home. Grace Bardot is a woman who no longer needs anything — no man, no friends, and certainly not the number of staff who work for her. She spends her days sipping gin and tonics in the sunshine while reading her favorite romance novels. The Bardot money is what they call *old money.* Because of Gran's parents, she's always lived a comfortable life, which afforded me one as well.

The car comes to a stop, and the back door whooshes open where we're met with the flashes of cameras, shouting press, and fans scream as my mother and father exit the vehicle. Stepping foot onto the plush red carpet, I attempt to ignore the shouts of my parents' names as we make our way through the crowd, stopping a few times to allow the cameras to capture us.

Finally, inside the enormous, gilded ballroom, my gaze flits around, hoping to find my best friend. It doesn't take long for me to spot the sleek, raven hair in the crowd. The only woman here with her hair not pinned with diamonds and pearls.

Leaving my folks to mingle, I make my way over to Aelin, who's already giggling up a storm with some dashing man in a three-piece suit. A dark tie leads up to a smooth, angular jaw, pale skin, and full, pink lips.

A squeal from beside me catches my attention before I meet his stare, and Aelin pulls me into a hug. "This is my best friend," she gushes, and I finally find the eyes of the man, no, actually, the boy she's talking to. He looks like he's younger than us.

"Nice to meet you," he tells me, offering a hand which I accept before side-eyeing Aelin.

"Can I talk to you?" I hiss at her. Glancing at the cute guy, I smile. "We'll catch you later." Pulling her through the crowd, we find the bar where I grab a flute of champagne for myself and one for her. "Are you crazy?"

"What?" Her wide, golden-brown orbs shimmer with amusement.

My gaze finds her boy-toy before I look at her again. "That guy isn't even old enough to drink yet." Rolling my eyes, I can't help but laugh when she giggles playfully.

"Oh come on, like you are? Also, I was having fun. His older brother is a hottie, so I did have a plan," she tells me conspiratorially. I sip my drink, allowing my gaze to rove the room, taking in the faces of the men and women who are all draped in designer clothes and exquisite jewels. Aelin's hand lands on my arm, her fingers wrapping around my wrist before she whisper-hisses, "Who is that?"

"Who?" I turn to where she's staring to be met with a man who looks like he's just stepped off the film set of some rough motorcycle club movie. He doesn't look like he fits in here with his leather jacket and black tee. His boots are dusty, his jeans fit too tight, hugging muscled thighs as he saunters deeper into the room. His midnight-black hair reminds me of my best friend's, and his tanned skin speaks of someone who's been outdoors in the full sun all day, every day.

Dangerous. That's the word to describe him.

"Now that is a man," Aelin murmurs more to herself than to me because I can't drag my gaze away. Menace emanates from him as if he were wearing it like a cologne. But then he makes a beeline for my father, which has my mouth dropping open in shock. The two men seem to know each other, but Dad pales when his gaze lands on the stranger. "Uhm..." My best friend's voice filters into nothing when my father disappears with said stranger into the hallway, talking heatedly as they go.

"Uhm, is right," I tell her, my attention now torn between catching up with Aelin or following Dad to find out what's going on. My gaze snaps back to where my mother seems completely oblivious to everything as she laughs and flirts with someone in a suit who looks like he's got one foot in the grave.

The emcee announces that dinner will soon be served and requests everyone to take their seats. All the while through dinner, Dad's face is a picture of pure dread. I lean over and whisper in his ear, "Are you okay?"

He chuckles. "Of course I am." The fake smile is back, lying to me directly to my face. It's the second time in my life he's done it, and my gut churns with unease. "Why don't you enjoy your dinner, sweetheart?" he tells me, nudging my chin with his knuckles in a gesture that usually would calm me down. But after what I've witnessed, it leaves a sinking feeling in my stomach.

LYCAN

The paperwork is in place. There's nowhere to run now because tonight, I'll be meeting *her*. I've been flicking through her social media for a few days now, taking in every photo I can. I've devoured her with my hungry ogling, and my predatory fangs are ready to sink into the sweet, supple flesh of Scarlett Bardot.

The one photo I've saved is of her in a beautiful red dress, the color of blood. The sleek, silky material hugs her curves like a second skin. Her long hair is draped over one shoulder in a thick, auburn braid. The thought of her with those flowing locks over her voluptuous tits makes my dick hard. She's not skinny, with curves enough to grip and manhandle, but even so, I'm certain she'll be able to bear children.

All I need is one son.

Horatio didn't know what he was setting his daughter up for when he walked into my world and wanted to play with the big boys. The dollar signs in his eyes flashed as he learned about everything that Heaven could gift him, a place to delve into the darkest fantasy, but also a place you could lose your soul to the devil. To me.

When Kahn arrived back from the gala, he told me exactly what Bardot had said; he gave Horatio the ultimatum. The payment will be his daughter's hand in marriage.

And then Kahn informed Horatio Bardot I will be bringing the contract to him personally. While we dine with the beauty, I'll assess her to ensure she's completely oblivious to who I am and why I'm there.

I should have been at the gala to hammer the final nail in the coffin, but having my right-hand man do it, allowing me time to prepare the contract, was necessary. And I wanted to meet Scarlett in her home for the first time. Not at some fancy party that had nothing to do with me.

Picking up the phone, I dial Alex's number. Two rings later, I hear his voice. "Do you have news for me?" The eagerness in his tone is the only giveaway that he's been waiting on me. It's only been a few days since he called, but Kahn and the team moved quickly.

"They walked into the convent, found a basement of fifteen girls, all new to the church. My men are looking into a chain of convents they'd been moved through posing as real churches. The nuns have young women join, all the while training them for more sinister futures. I have a few names. One, in particular, stands out."

"Lorenzo?" Alex asks, naming the person in question, no surprise in his tone. He knew we'd find it. He knew I would send Kahn to do this job, and that's why he called me.

"You realize this is going to blow up before the month is at its end?" I lean back in my chair, ignoring the paperwork I need to get through before dinner tonight. I have a couple of hours, but I'm intrigued to know why Alex really allowed me to take the lead with this.

"That's the idea. Once the Cartel knows we're onto them, we'll have started a blood war. Something I'm looking forward to because I want that man's life in my hands, and when I finally get it, I'll ensure to snuff it out."

And there it is, the underlying promise. There's nothing I've ever done for the mafia that didn't come with another hidden agenda, and this time it's no different. I should feel used, but I enjoy when justice is found.

"My man taking the lead on this won't stop

until he's found Lorenzo," I tell Alex. "If he does…"

"I know. It's not Lorenzo I want. Tell your team they have permission to take what they need, a pound of flesh, or more, but I want the leader."

Chuckling, I shake my head at his passion. Once, long ago, that was me. When they took my father's life, and my brother sided with them instead of his blood. That's why Darius and I no longer see eye to eye. He believed their lies about our father, and I, being the eldest son, took on the responsibility left to me. "You'll get him. My men won't step on any toes. I can assure you of that, Carnevali."

"Good. I'm flying home tonight. I may have to visit Heaven for an evening of decadent play before I get back to LA." I can hear the smile in his voice. The temptation of spending a few hours in my club's exclusive back rooms has become a staple to most Made Men in this city.

"I'm not in New York for another few days, but when you're at JFK, let me know. I'll have one of my cars collect you and bring you straight to the club. You can have a quiet evening, or you can choose any one of the women who are regulars."

"Only one?" He laughs, and I realize he's always been one to partake in a ménage scene, or even three women, with him enjoying the spoils.

"Well, you know you're welcome to anything in any one of my clubs." Pushing to my feet, I grab my jacket, realizing the time. "I have to head out. Important meeting tonight, and I can't be late."

"Of course. See you soon," Alex tells me before hanging up, leaving me to my thoughts of this evening's festivities. Pocketing my cell phone, I grab my keys and wallet before leaving the office, locking the door behind me. When I reach the club floor, I find Sawyer, one of the men working with Kahn.

The tall, ex-marine has been with me for almost five years, learning the ins and outs of the underground export business the Shaw name runs. When I took over from my father, I knew I needed men I could trust.

"Mr. Shaw," he greets when I near him as he settles himself on a stool at the bar. The club isn't busy, a handful of clients have made themselves comfortable in the booths, and the sleek, silver bar, which curves like a horseshoe, is empty but for Sawyer.

"I'm heading back to Crimson Falls," I tell him. "Can you stay to close up?"

He nods. "Of course." There's a rigidness to him, cold, closed off, and I wonder briefly if he's ever had the love of a woman. He doesn't play in the club, he's never mentioned coming home from Iraq to anyone, and when we've spent time together in meetings with the team, his focus has been laser sharp no matter which of the women I employ

21

would stroll in, needing something from me.

"Good." I move past him, making my way to the garage where my shiny, raven-colored Cadillac Escalade waits. I settle back in the driver's seat as I start the engine, and the speakers play a soft melody. The gentle voice of Ruelle comes through as she sings "Find You" and I can't help but smile.

It's time to meet my future wife. Only, she doesn't know about me. She doesn't realize her life is about to change.

The streets are busy for this late, but I glide through the city as I take the highway out to Seattle's northern suburbs, where Bardot lives with his family. A man with the means to live anywhere in the world, but he chooses *my* city. As much as I love the Big Apple, it's only one of many venues I consider elite. Seattle has taken my heart and allowed me to play when I need to without having to form long-term connections with women.

But Horatio is one of the reasons I haven't left Seattle yet. He knew what he was doing when he bought the house just outside the bustling metropolis. The fact that my father trusted him angers me. The fact that he took from me only infuriates me further. The money he took hardly made a dent in my fortune; however, when someone takes something of mine, I believe it's only fair to claim something of theirs in repayment.

I'm pulling up to the Bardot mansion's wrought iron gates when my phone rings through the speakers. "Yes?" I answer, knowing it's Kahn calling with news, and by the time the car winds up the long, paved driveway leading to a three-story house, my focus is on my eagerness to meet Scarlett Bardot.

"I stumbled upon something you might want to know before you walk into the Bardot house tonight," he tells me, his voice tense, the clipped tone of his words warning me that I'm not going to like the outcome of his investigations.

Hitting the brakes, I say, "Tell me everything."

SCARLETT

I haven't been able to talk to Dad since the night of the charity gala. He's been gone for a few days, and tonight is the first time he's been home. The man he was talking to still has me on edge because I have no idea who he was. The stranger didn't fit in, and he never returned when Dad did, which means the stranger was sent away.

Only, I'm not sure if it was a friendly parting or not.

Classical music drifts from the dining room as I make my way down the stairs. My parents must have guests over because I hear glasses clinking together and my mother's laughter at something someone said. Whenever we have guests, it's always like this. She puts on a show in front of them, but by the time they leave, she and Dad are at each other's throats.

The moment my sneakers hit the expensive Italian tiles, my mother's voice rings out to me. "Scarlett, come in here for a moment, darling." The fake tone of her voice has me rolling my eyes.

My twenty-first birthday is coming up, and I told her I wanted to spend my summer with Gran before I fly to New York to start my internship. The excitement at finally moving out on my own has taken over, and I've been counting down the days until I'm free. Spending my life behind the opulent walls of the Bardot mansion has been stifling, and I'm more than ready to find my independence.

It's been difficult to accept that my future had been planned for me, even before I could walk. Just last year, my mother was convinced I would be married by the time I'm twenty-one, but she soon learned my desire was to work hard, build a company from the ground up, and not depend on a man to pay for everything.

I reach our lavish entertainment area, which leads into the dining room and take it in. Decked in furniture which cost more than most people make in a year and dripping with a gilded chandelier, I find my parents both dressed to the nines, along with a man I've never met before.

The moment I enter the room, his gaze snaps

to mine, stealing the breath from my lungs at the luminosity of the jade color. A seemingly nonchalant glimpse lands on me, locking on mine, reminding me of the vacations Dad used to take me on to British Columbia. The lake house we had overlooked a thick forest, which was as dangerous as this man's stare. The stranger's dark hair matches his charcoal suit. The danger that he seems to exude fills the room with menace, but I tip my chin up, showing him an act of defiance. My mother and father may cower to the wealthy assholes who walk in here, but I won't. My gaze tracks his silver button-up shirt because I need a reprieve from his intensity, but it doesn't help distract me because his body is immaculate in form.

Everything about this man seems put together for a reason. He doesn't wear something for the sake of covering up. It's been chosen specifically for him to lord over the people he's around. His presence screams wealth, and when he looks at me, the corner of his mouth quirks slightly as if I amuse him.

The heat in his gaze burns me from head to toe as he regards my outfit—sneakers, a black lace tank top, along with a pair of frayed denim shorts. My long, red hair has been straightened to the middle of my back, and my makeup is nonexistent since I didn't expect us to have company.

"There you are," my mother says, a smile plastered on her face as she takes in my appearance with a slight scowl before she pastes on the fake smile. "Come here." Her hand waves toward me, gesturing for me to close the distance, but with every step I take, the more I *feel* the stranger's eyes raking over me. It's almost as if he's touching me.

"Scarlett, this is Mr. Shaw," Dad says, introducing the stranger to me. "He's having dinner with us this evening." There's a hint of tension in my father's voice, but he offers me a smile, which sets me at ease for the moment, but something else niggles at me. My dad is formidable, but the air in the room is thick with foreboding.

The man in question, Mr. Shaw, locks his cool gaze on me and offers me a smile. His hand extends toward me. The moment I slip my fingers along his palm, electric currents shoot through my arm, but I can't pull away because his hold is like solid steel.

"It's lovely to meet you, Scarlett," he says, allowing my name to roll off his tongue like the smooth whiskey he's drinking. His deep baritone and slight accent I can't quite put my finger on, send tingles of awareness right through me—from the top of my head to the tips of my toes.

"Same here," I answer in a whisper before he releases my hand and allows me to step back. The scent of him hangs in the air—cigars, and cinnamon. It is a strange combination, nothing like anyone I've come across before, especially since my dad and none of the men he considers friends have ever smoked in this house.

"Shall we?" Mom breaks the silence with a nervous grin, and we all follow her to the dining room table, where I notice four places have been set. I didn't plan on sitting with them, but it seems my presence is needed.

I settle in beside Mom as she slides her chair forward. The two men take their seats, Dad, at the head of the table, while Mr. Shaw settles in opposite me. Even though I'm not usually a nervous person, this man sets my stomach tumbling as he takes me in. It's almost as if he's assessing me for something.

Dinner is served moments later. The fragrance of spicy tomato soup and fresh, warm bread fills my nostrils, but even that can't wash away the scent of Mr. Shaw.

"Tell me, Scarlett," he speaks as I lift the spoon, scooping up the red liquid. "What is it you would like to accomplish in life, or better yet, what is your career choice?" Intrigue glints in his eye. Assessing me, he smiles, tipping his head to the side, and I wonder if he does it so he doesn't look as scary. But it only makes him seem more sinister in his appraisal of me. He reminds me of a dangerous animal, watching its prey, stalking until it's time to strike.

My gaze holds his for a moment before I focus

on his mouth as he takes the spoon to his lips. The wetness from the soup causes a gentle glisten to capture and hold my attention. The deep red color reminds me of blood and just how predatorily he looks as he swallows, his tongue darting out to savor the taste of his kill. His throat works, the Adam's apple under smooth, tanned skin has my body doing strange things. I've never really watched a man like I'm doing with him, and I'm not sure why.

"Scarlett?" Mother's cool tone brings me back to the present, and I clear my throat, casting her a quick glance.

"Yes, sorry. I'd like to hopefully open my own media agency," I tell him with confidence brimming in my tone. "The need for honest reporting is something that has become somewhat of a passion of mine. What do you do?" My inquiry causes him to chuckle, the sound low, rumbling through his chest, and I wonder what's so funny.

"I don't think little girls should be so curious," he tells me, then sips another mouthful of his soup, but each movement he makes sends heat through me, and I can't explain why. His use of the term *little girl* rankles me, but I don't bite because he's trying to annoy me. I can tell with how he's watching, waiting for me to take the bait.

He's handsome, classically so, with sharp features and a jawbone free of stubble, but there is a dark shadow over the otherwise olive skin, which tells me if he doesn't shave, there'd be a beautifully thick beard. His lips form a tempting cupid's bow, with the lower lip fatter than the top. A mouth I'm sure could do sinful things if given a chance.

I'm not overly experienced, but I know enough to recognize a man who can make women swoon with a mere glance. His dark brow arches, and I realize I'm staring again. Shaking my head, I drop my gaze and eat my soup in silence, unsure of how to take him. Or even why I'm here in the first place.

"And you're planning on running it all by yourself?" he asks, and I *feel* his stare on me once more. The heat of it captures me, and I nod. "Words, little girl."

"I'm not a little girl," I bite out through gritted teeth, shoving my bowl away in frustration. "I'm twenty. I'm an adult."

This causes him to chuckle, his head angled as he regards me with amusement. "Oh?"

"Scarlett!" My mother's tone turns my name into a curse word. Her heated glare is scorching me, but I don't look at her. I'm staring at the man before me.

"Yes," I answer back, causing him to laugh once more. "It's not funny. I'll be twenty-one in a month, and when I complete my internship, I'll have the necessary experience to start my own business. And

I'll be able to do anything a man can do, possibly even better." Folding my arms across my chest, I don't turn my attention away from Mr. Shaw.

He sits back, and I don't miss the way his gaze flicks to my chest before meeting my stare as he regards me, the corners of his mouth upturned. His hands rest on the table, fingers tangled in between each other, and a thought of just how they'd feel touching me sparks through me for a split second before he speaks. "I like your fire, little red." His tone holds what I can only deem respect with fire blazing in his eyes. "It's refreshing. Most women cower in my presence," he continues, pushing to his feet, which has both my folks standing as well.

But I don't. Instead, I sit in my chair, my arms crossed as I watch his next move.

"Thank you for dinner, folks," he says in a bright tone, which belies the darkness swirling in those forest depths because his gaze never strays from me. "I'll have to get going if I'm going to catch the early flight to New York."

"Of course, I'm so sorry you have to leave so soon," Mom coos as if she's about to kiss his shoes as he leaves our house. "Let us walk you out. I have to apologize for Scarlett. She's feeling anxious about her future."

"There's no need for that," Shaw says before stopping at my chair, his hand landing on the back of it, but I feel the brush of his knuckles against my skin. He leans in, his lips a hair's breadth away from my cheek, and he whispers, "The big bad wolf won't eat you if you don't veer off the path."

I turn my head, branding him with my stare. "That's a fairy tale told to little girls to scare them."

Those deep, jade gemstones take in my sleek strands before he shrugs. "Perhaps. But little girls should always be wary of predators hunting for sweet, supple flesh," he says. "Especially when they go visit Grandma." He straightens as I shoot to my feet, but he's walking off before I have time to focus on what he's just said.

"Wait," I call, but all he does is offer me a wave as he makes his way to the exit where my parents are cowing to him as if he were the fucking King of England, and they were mere peasants.

I don't know who he is, but his attempt to scare me won't work.

I'm not a little girl afraid of the big bad wolf.

At least, that's what I tell myself.

LYCAN

The plane touches down on the East Coast, and I'm already anxious to get back and see *her*. The private hangar is empty apart from my men, who seem to have taken it upon themselves to ensure I have two cars waiting for me. When I built *my* empire from the ground up, there was only one thing I knew I needed to do, and that was to ensure my brother never came near me again. Being in New York sets me on edge because I know he's not far.

Our father left me with the export business, but I created Shaw Industries and made it what it is today—a sought-after conglomerate that would make the wealthiest men weep. With hotels and nightclubs, exclusive BDSM venues, and even a security company that would seed out the most hidden secrets, men come to me to *fix* what they broke. Kahn and his team have ensured I can vouch for them without blinking, and that's what I wanted, something to be proud of. With my plans to open a string of BDSM clubs across the country and then the world, I knew I needed to come to the New York branch to ensure everything is running smoothly.

But the thought of Darius on the loose sets me on edge. My brother isn't someone I can rely on or trust. With me being someone who runs his business with an iron fist, I don't doubt some of the men I've let go over the past few months have found him and ensured he knows my every move. But I'm not afraid. I've never been scared of him, and he knows it.

I should be back in Washington, where *she* is, but I needed to face the team here in person. Once I'm done, I'll fly back and find my little red when she visits grandma in Crimson Falls and claim what is rightfully mine. The fire she exuded certainly left me hard for her all night. I didn't want to walk away from her and come out here, but offering her a false sense of security will ensure she won't see me coming.

They've always called me the hunter and my brother the wolf, but I became both somewhere down the line. When the Bardots fucked me over with Horatio stealing money from me, I showed them I'm not some pushover they could fuck with. And now, their beautiful yet feisty daughter's hand in marriage is my payment.

After meeting her last night, I'm certainly intrigued by the young woman. She may be young, but she's exquisite. The way she carries herself captured my attention and every inch of her sweet curves tempted me enough to keep me interested.

What she doesn't know is that her life has already been planned out. It's sweet she thinks she'll be opening her own business. When I'm done with her, she'll be in my bed, pregnant with my heirs. At thirty-nine, I know I have to get started on a family who will be there one day when I'm gone. That's why I wanted someone younger, someone supple and sweet.

As I make my way to the car and slip onto the bench seat, my driver takes his place and starts the engine. His gaze meets mine in the rearview mirror, awaiting my command.

"I'll be going to Hawthorne first," I tell him, and he nods as we pull out of the parking area. I reach for my phone in my breast pocket and find it buzzing wildly. "What?"

"We've spotted Darius. He's on a bike heading out of Miami."

"Keep a tail on him. I don't need him disappearing again." I hang up before they can give me any excuses. My brother thinks he can outsmart me, but I have more money than god, which is what he walked away from, and it also gives me the upper hand.

Flicking open my app list, I scroll down to the one I need and open her profile—no new photos or posts. The last one she put up was of her in that god-awful black and denim ensemble she wore to dinner. The top itself wasn't bad, the lace offering a hint of what's beneath, but other than that, I'm going to have to get her to dress appropriately since she'll be on my arm at all the events I attend.

When I told her to be wary of the big bad wolf, I wasn't joking. She didn't need to know the finer details just yet. I can't wait to get my new bride to my home. The house in Crimson Falls, my father's stately property, will be ready for her.

The fact that her new home will not be far from her grandmother's house is convenient. Since it's right next door to the Bardot mansion is a testament to just how far I'll go to get her and keep her. I thought about buying somewhere else, a new city or town, but I know throwing money around isn't going to be the way to ensure her compliance.

I want her submission in every way possible, and there's no doubt in my mind she's going to be a challenge.

When we pull up to the building, I glance out

of the window, taking note of the bustling streets. The door opens, and I step out, offering my driver a nod before I button my suit jacket and head into the awaiting, gleaming foyer.

Gold shimmers from the chandelier hanging from the center of the ceiling, offering a glittering entrance as you walk into the apartment block. An upmarket position within the city, wealthy patrons dripping from head to toe in designer labels pricing that most would balk at. Well, when I say most, I mean anyone who isn't me.

"Good evening, sir." The receptionist grins. I run this place like a hotel. You can't rent an apartment long-term, and most of the clientele only need a month or two.

"Is everything ready?"

A soft blush turns her cheeks pink, but the dark-haired beauty doesn't capture my attention like Scarlett. There's no fire. She's far too submissive and compliant. Which has me wondering if that's what my little red would be once I've broken her in. That won't do. I like fire. I love to be burned by my choices. It makes the challenge that much more exciting.

"Yes, sir," she responds and leans over her desk to offer me a glimpse of her cleavage, which looks like it's about to spill from the dress. "It's nice to see you again."

"I'm sure it is." I turn on my heel and head to the private elevator that will take me up to the rooftop club. It's an exclusive, well-known slice of heaven, and when the car deposits me outside the sleek, black doors, I twist the silver handle and step into every Dominant's fantasy.

Women kneel beside their Masters, and some even have two submissives who obediently await their next orders. Some have male submissives; others have a mix of male and female. When I first opened Heaven, I planned for it to be exclusively for my staff, for those who lived the lifestyle, but over time, it became something of a gem that people paid an extortionate amount of money for.

People like Bardot and his wife. Only, she no longer wanted this life, and he, on the other hand, took it upon himself to partake in the festivities when she didn't know. The more money he needed to pay his membership fees, the more money he stole from me.

Now, he'd do anything to ensure my silence. Hence the reason I have a new bride to take care of when I get back. But for now, I move through the space, heading toward the viewing rooms.

"Mr. Shaw," a voice drifts over the soft, classical music that plays in the background, and I turn to find Kahn. The businesses I run are varied, and he's one of the soldiers I send in to extricate information when needed.

"How are you doing?" I glance over my shoulder, taking him in. He's worked for me for several years after leaving the marines, but I know there's more to him than meets the eye. His file told me so, even if he didn't. It took him a while to admit his reasons for wanting this job. One being the income, but the other, focus. He knows about my resources and connections. His sister was taken just after he returned home, and he's been looking for her ever since. I don't mind him using my resources for it, but I wish he'd tell me.

I'm not a complete monster. I hope he finds her.

"I'm good. There's been some talk about the priest moving down to NOLA after we cleared the girls from the one Carnevali mentioned," he tells me as we stand side by side, watching a scene play out before us. A submissive getting her face fucked roughly, spit running down her chin as tears stream down her flushed cheeks. Her body merely a plaything for the man using her.

Pleasure is written all over his face, and I imagine having Scarlett in that exact position. I turn away, needing to calm down before I jump on the plane and head back to see her. Meeting Kahn's gaze, I inquire, "And you'd like to sort that out for me?"

"I would." It's his way of telling me he needs

this. There's something more going down at the church with Father Lorenzo and his flock. "He's been on my radar for a long time, and there's someone there I'd like to ensure is safe."

I'll gladly allow him to fly out tonight to kill Lorenzo before the good Father steals more girls off the streets.

"Tell me something, Kahn," I speak. "Does this have anything to do with the real reason you agreed to work for me?"

His gaze snaps to mine, and he nods. He knows that I know. If he were someone I didn't respect, I would kill him right here, in front of everyone, and make sure people fear me. But for now, I'll allow him to do what he needs to.

"Go. When you get back, I need to know everything."

"Yes, sir." He offers a salute before disappearing. Now that I've sorted him out, I make my way to the private room where I have a redhead waiting for me. She's not Scarlett, but she'll have to do.

SCARLETT

By the time I reach my grandmother's estate, I'm exhausted. The small town she lives in, Crimson Falls, Washington, is nothing more than a vast forested area with a few exclusive homes dotted within the trees. Hidden like a rare jewel, it sits amongst the tall pine trees, usually in clouds, with a light drizzle that can continue for days on end.

As the car draws nearer to the large estate, anticipation trickles down my spine like a snake slithering across the ground. The memory of Mr. Shaw's words sends a cold shiver through me, which shakes me to the bone.

It's been so long since I visited, but I knew it was time to see the old lady and spend time with her. She's getting on in age, and from what Mom says, she's not doing all that great. I'm also here to help her with the annual Bardot Ball that raises money for children abandoned by their parents or orphaned. The event sees guests drive up just for the evening, but there's another worry that's twisting my gut. *Would Mr. Shaw be in attendance?*

After he left, my parents told me he's going to be around a lot more. I'm not sure why, or in what capacity, but they both seemed afraid of the prospect, which doesn't sit well with me. As handsome as I find him, there is something sinister that sparks in his gaze.

We come to a stop just outside the mansion. The building is three floors of pure opulence. Wealth drips from every corner of my grandmother's house, and as much as I'd rather be at home, it's a reprieve from sitting and listening to my mother telling me what a disappointment I am.

The driver opens my door before offering me his hand, which I accept. The moment I step foot on the soft soil, awareness of being watched slithers over me. It feels as if there are eyes on me, waiting in the shadows. But as I turn to look out at the long driveway, taking in the trees surrounding the estate, I don't see anything in the darkness. It's late, nearing nine in the evening, and after the long day, I'm exhausted.

"Miss Bardot," Ellington, my driver, calls to get

my attention. "I'll get the bags," he tells me. "Please wait at the door for me."

Nodding, I offer him a smile before making my way toward the large, ornate entrance that beckons. With a wrought iron handle and knocker, the dark wooden door sends more cold awareness through me.

This will be my home for the next four weeks. As much as I wanted space from my parent's constant bickering, the ghostly feel of the property makes the hairs on the back of my neck stand on end.

The rumors of Gran's deteriorating mental capacity have been whispers I grew up with, and I have a feeling that's why my parents agreed to me visiting her. Perhaps they want this stupid ball to go off without a hitch, so the Bardot name isn't tarnished. That's all they care about anyway, and that's the reason they sent me instead of coming themselves.

With my last name, I'm known throughout the country as the most eligible bachelorette, but even though my reputation precedes me, I'm still single— much to my mother's disgrace.

By the time I turn twenty-one, I should be married with children, at least according to my mother. The traditions that run in my family are archaic. Even though we're in the twenty-first century, they seem to think we're still living in the middle ages.

"Here you are." Ellington's voice causes me to jump as he walks up behind me. "I'm sorry, miss," he apologizes with a tepid smile. I watch as he pushes the door open, and a loud creak of annoyance comes from the hinges as it gapes, welcoming me inside.

Shockingly, the house is warmer than I expected when I enter. The marble tiles underfoot echo with the click of my heels. The long, deep-red-and-brown rug that lies in a straight line leading up to a sweeping spiral staircase gifts the enormous space with a hint of balminess.

I wonder if there's a heating system of sorts, but my grandmother would never pay for this place to be kept heated if I had to guess correctly. A heavy chandelier hangs above me, with crystals glinting in the dim light.

"Hello." A voice comes from my right, forcing me to turn toward a doorway that leads off from the foyer. "Welcome to Bardot Manor." A woman who looks to be in her mid-forties smiles at me brightly.

"Thank you," I respond. "I'm—"

"Scarlett Bardot," she says, interrupting me. "We've been so excited to have you visit. I hope you had a lovely trip?"

"Yes, it was acceptable," I tell her before glancing around once more.

Ellington offers me a nod before tipping his

black driver's hat at us and exiting, shutting the heavy door behind him. And that's the final nail in my proverbial coffin. Once the car leaves, I'm stuck here.

"Let me show you to your room," the woman, who I still don't know, says.

I place a hand on her arm, needing her to look at me before I ask, "What is your name?"

She gushes, holding her hand to her chest. "I'm so sorry. How rude of me. I'm Estelle," she informs me before curtsying as if I were the queen and she a mere servant. It seems Gran has taught the staff to bow down to her. I'm not surprised.

"No need for formality. I'm not my grandmother." Before Estelle can respond, I head toward the staircase and take a few steps up before turning to see the woman following without my bags.

"I'll have Gray bring those up shortly."

"Thank you." I face the staircase, and when Estelle reaches me, she turns left, and I follow. The hallway is carpeted with thick, dark brown material that allows us to move silently, the plushness quieting our footsteps as she takes me all the way to the end and pushes open a dark wooden door. The bedroom ahead is prepared with fresh flowers in a vase on the vanity made of dark, rich oak, sitting looking over the enormous four-poster bed, draped in what looks like fresh bed linens. The pillows are the color of deep merlot, and the comforter a similar dark red.

"This will be your wing of the house. Your grandmother is on the other end. You're welcome to explore on your own, but just be wary of going out into the garden after dark." Her voice is tainted with a dark threat that has me snapping my gaze toward her.

"Why?" I question, waiting for her response. For a moment, I wonder if she's going to reply, and I turn away, allowing her privacy rather than gawking at her. I open the curtain to look out over the lawn's lush greenery and flowerbeds with bright leaves shimmering with water droplets under spotlights that illuminate the beauty that awaits me tomorrow morning.

The bright colors of the petals—reds, yellows, oranges, and even purple—are so pronounced under the glow I can make them out easily. A pathway leads toward thick forests that further extends to a mountain that looks like a large, black mound. The forest ahead reminds me of those I read as a girl in dark fairy tales. "There aren't any big bad wolves out there."

"Oh, no, not at all. We just have the gardener working at night. He sets the traps for the foxes who attempt to make a play for the chickens in the coop.

It can be dangerous if you don't know where they are."

"And he does this at night?" I spin on my heel, looking at the older woman. *Why would someone want to do that at night?* It's rather strange.

"Yes, he feels it's better than doing it in the day; that way, we can explore the gardens safely while the sun is up," Estelle says as she waves her hand in the air as if she thinks it's as silly as I do.

"I see. And how old is he?" My curiosity piques at the thought of someone wandering alone at night in the shadows, lurking outside my window.

Her gaze snaps to mine at the question, her eyes wide as she regards me. "Oh, he's not for you, sweet Scarlett. You stay clear of him."

Her words have me laughing out loud. "I'm not at all interested in a man who works in a garden setting traps, I can assure you of that." I shake my head with a grin. Knowing that when I get home, I'll have a multitude of bachelors waiting for me, and it will all be my mother's doing.

Her brows furrow at my words, but she doesn't respond. Estelle only offers a curt nod before she heads for the door. Her reaction to me is strange, and I wonder if I've offended her by what I said.

"Good night, Miss Bardot. I trust you'll sleep well," she greets before walking out of the room, leaving me staring at the empty space. I want to close it, but only moments later, an older gentleman brings my suitcases, and I guess it's Gray.

"Good evening, Miss. Bardot," he says, as he pulls the suitcases through the door and sets them down on a stool near the closet.

I watch him for a moment, before enquiring, "You're Gray?"

"Yes, ma'am." He nods with a gentlemanly bow.

"Tell me something, Gray." I turn to face him fully, watching as he straightens to full height. "The gardener who works for Gran. Is there something I should know about him?"

The old man's eyes widen as he regards me. "I… I think perhaps you should meet him yourself, ma'am," he tells me, his voice shaking as he speaks, which only sets my curiosity alight.

He doesn't say anything more, pulling the door shut behind him, leaving me with even more questions than I had before. The house is large, and I'm excited to explore. It's been a long time since I've been here, and with the multitude of rooms, I wonder just what could be hiding within the walls, or more so, outside the walls of Bardot House.

I cast my glance out of the window once more, taking in the darkness, and as a shadow passes across the lawn, my heart leaps against my rib cage, and I can't drag my gaze away from the large figure.

When he stops, I notice his head twist, eyes

landing on me, as if he can see me in the darkness. I can't make out what he looks like, but he seems more beast than man as he watches me. The whites of his eyes burn through the darkness, and I have to move away from the window, my breath coming in short spurts of nervous air.

There's something very peculiar about him. About the shadow in the garden, but perhaps it's my mind playing tricks on me. Sighing, I move to the suitcases and promise to get ready for bed. Exhaustion takes over, and I know tomorrow, in the light of the sun, I'll be able to explore better.

SCARLETT

When my eyes open, there's no sunshine streaming through the window. Instead, I'm met with the dire grayness of clouds hanging heavily in the sky. The house seems more haunted, with the weather turning somber than it would if the golden glow of the day were shimmering inside.

I quickly dress in a skirt with a sweater that warms me. Even though the heating is on, there's still a chill in the air when I open my bedroom door. The moment I step foot in the kitchen, the chef and Estelle stop speaking and turn to regard me.

"Good morning, sweet Scarlett." The old lady grins happily. "This is Jean-Pierre; he's the full-time chef at Bardot House."

"Nice to meet you," I tell the older gentleman

who's dressed in a proper chef's uniform.

His face crinkles when he smiles. "Ma cherie," he says with a tip of his head before turning his attention back to the stove.

"Are you hungry?" Estelle asks, moving swiftly toward me. "I've set out breakfast for you in the dining room. Your grandmother said she'll be back in a few days. She had business in the city, so she'll be gone for a little while."

"Oh." Disappointment squeezes in my chest, stealing the words from my lips. I was hoping to see her, spend some time with her before the ball. It's been a few years since my gran and I were able to sit and talk, to catch up on the news of what I've been doing.

"Don't worry," Estelle mumbles as she leads me through the dining room entrance, and I find myself in a familiar room. When I was much younger, I recall being in here for lunch with the rest of the family. Sitting at the long, twelve-seater table always felt as if we were royals. "She'll be back soon enough."

I'm seated at the head of the table, gifting me a view of the room, and then I'm left alone with what looks like a buffet set out for a princess. Fruits that shine as if they'd been polished, freshly made toast, eggs, and sausages, along with juice and a French Press of steaming coffee. I start with that, pouring myself a mug full and heading toward the window to take in the view.

With the weather being so dismal, I think I'll have to stay indoors and read. If I recall correctly, my grandmother's library is filled with classics as well as some intriguing volumes of the ancestors who first moved to Crimson Falls.

Sipping my drink, I watch two staff heading to what looks like a vegetable patch at the far side of the kitchen. They both carry baskets, and begin filling them with greens, which I'm sure will be used for dinner tonight.

I settle in the chair and fill my plate with delicious smelling food. The silence of the house is startling, the clinking of the cutlery is the only sound, and I wonder if spending a month here was a mistake because I do like to have someone to talk to or music to listen to. I'm sure Gran won't mind me using her music room, but it's going to be lonely all by myself.

With the ball a week away, I'm sure she'll be in attendance, but with her running Bardot Industries, she may not stick around if she didn't even want to greet me before leaving this morning.

Loneliness seeps through me like a rabid poison.

Growing up with my folks who were more interested in spending time with their friends, I've learned to be alone, but there are times it becomes too much. Perhaps I can call Aelin to come to visit for a few days. She'd love it here.

Once I've finished eating, I head toward the kitchen only to find it empty. Furrowing my brow, I turn and make my way through the house, taking a long hallway toward the library, which I remember as a girl. The room hasn't changed much. The walls are lined with shelves of uncracked spines, calling to me to explore. An enormous open-brick fireplace sits against one wall, which has a large grandfather clock above the mantle.

A three-seater couch with matching armchairs furnish the middle of the room, surrounding a thick brown throw rug and a knee-height coffee table. On the smooth surface, I spy a few magazines, mostly home improvement ones, which don't interest me.

I allow my gaze to take in the bookshelves, tracing my finger over the smooth spines. Some are old, first editions, others are newer, with sleek glossy covers, and I can't help but giggle at some of the romances she's collected over the years. I find an old copy of fairy tales. The one of Red Riding Hood piques my interest, and I slide it out.

The cover doesn't have an image; instead, the title is engraved in gold on the dark green jacket. I flick it open and find a handwritten note, which I scan with furrowed brows.

My darling, Grace,
As the wolf loves his damsel, so I love you.
Yours always,
C.S.

I'm not sure who C.S. is, but I must ask my gran when she returns. My grandad died before I met him, but his name was Randolf Thurston. I recall Gran telling me she would never take another man's name, and that's why she was always Grace Bardot.

It must be an old friend. It's a beautiful gift. She's always loved the old stories by the Grimm Brothers instead of the newer, less scary retellings.

Settling in one of the amber leather armchairs, I curl my legs under my butt and open the book.

A sound startles me, causing the book I'd fallen asleep holding to tumble to the floor. Another heavy crunch sends my mind reeling. The room is now drenched in black, and I glance at the fireplace where a clock hangs above the mantle. I'm not sure if the hands are correct, but if they are, I've slept most of the day away.

It's almost six, which means dinner will probably be served soon. Pushing to my feet, I move to the window, wanting to find the sound that woke me, but all I see are shadows in the garden ahead. A shiver takes hold of me, and I force my sleepy body up the stairs to my bedroom to find a hoodie. Perhaps some fresh air will help me wake up.

I still can't believe I spent my first day in Crimson Falls asleep. In my room, I discard the sweater I'd been wearing and grab the red hoodie and pull it on over my T-shirt. Donning the hood to cover my hair, I race down the stairs and out the patio doors onto the stoop, which is hard beneath my sneakers.

Light streams from the spotlights, illuminating the garden just like they did last night. A howl from somewhere in the forest has a gasp falling from my lips. There isn't any staff outside, but I should be safe since Estelle told me there are traps for any foxes wanting to get onto the property.

I take one step off the stoop onto the lush grass, which feels as if I'm walking on a cloud.

A sound to the left of where I'm standing startles me, and I wonder if the gardener is outside doing work. "Hello?" I call out, but there isn't any response. Shrugging, I move farther into the garden, to where I recall two of the staff picking vegetables this morning. The patch is dimly lit, and I can make out a few types of lettuce and some carrots which have been pulled out. I don't recognize a few other plants, and I make a mental note to ask Jean-Pierre about them.

A branch cracking has me whipping my head behind me, but I don't see anyone there. The hair on the back of my neck stands on end when I hear another scrape of what I can only guess is a shoe against concrete. My gaze snaps to the stoop, but there's nobody there either.

"If you're trying to scare me, it's not working!" I call out to who I can only guess is the gardener attempting to freak me out. Shaking my head, I move toward the house, and that's when I see a large figure at the door. A scream is stuck in my throat when he moves slowly, predatorially toward me.

I can't see his face properly, but from the shadows, I can tell he must be at least six-five with broad shoulders, and he's wearing a dark hoodie that covers his face. Then I notice the glint of a blade in his hand. And that's when I race through the garden.

LYCAN

Being back in Crimson Falls is intriguing, but also, I'm anxious to get this contract in motion. The home I grew up in, the one where my memories now lie, is where I'll bring her. Even though I haven't been here in a long time, I know it will be the perfect place for me to ensure my little red is safe while she comes to terms with her new life.

The flight back from New York was quick, and the drive up here was refreshing. A change from the city. The furnishings my decorator chose are exquisite—all dark woods, glass and steel in the kitchen, and claret carpets overlying the expensive marble tiles.

I head up the sweeping staircase and turn left down the hall to the room I've had set up for Scarlett.

Upon pushing open the door, I find the ornate four-poster bed, a myriad of cushions, and a deep red comforter.

On the opposite side of the bed is a vanity with a beautifully intricate mirror. Carved from the finest oak, the frame shows a little girl with a red hood and the wolf right behind her. They've painted the hood perfectly, her long hair hanging over her shoulders as the predator makes his way toward her.

Reaching for the sculpted scene, I trace my finger over the hood, the memory of Scarlett's sleek, red hair flickering in my mind. The length perfect for fisting around my hand, her eyes wide and bright as she regarded me with fire and defiance. My cock jolts with the memory, and I can't help but grin. How perfectly delicious it will be to break her down and watch her submit to my whims.

When I planned to bring her here, I wanted the room to feel like home. Even though she's going to hate me for a while, I figure at least she can hate in comfort. The contract I signed with her father ensures she's mine and no longer a Bardot. She will be a Shaw as soon as the ceremony is complete.

A man relinquishing his hold on his daughter because he fucked up is a sad state of affairs. But he did it to ensure I never divulged what he did behind his wife's back. Yes, she knew about the money, the club, but she I'm certain has no clue her husband has a much larger secret, one that would most certainly break the perfect family unit he's managed to build.

Power has been my drug for a long time. I've reveled in it. Knowing I have the command to take down anyone who steps in my path is a heady feeling. Dominance goes hand in hand with the emotion, and I can't wait to see Scarlett on the other end of my control.

A smile slowly moves along my face, one that isn't filled with humor, but a sinister need to have her here right now. I have time, but I'd like it sooner rather than later. When the Bardot ball takes place, she will be on my arm. And if she tries to escape, I'll lock her up in this palace until she submits fully, in every way possible. Another grin graces my lips at the thought, this one filled with dark humor.

"Mr. Shaw," the voice of the man I put in the Bardot home to keep an eye on my new possession calls to me, causing me to return to the present. "I've met her," he says as he enters her bedroom, where I'm still standing over the vanity.

"And?" I turn, facing him as he moves deeper into the room. I've known Gray since I was a child. From the moment I realized I would never have a normal life, he was there for me. He's been good to me, obeying my commands without question.

He nods slowly, a small beam of happiness on his face, and for a moment, I think he's going to tell me not to do this, but then he says, "She's beautiful, I have to admit. You will make a wonderful couple. But there's something you do need to know."

"What is it, Gray?" The frustration in my tone has him wincing, and I have a feeling whatever it is he has to tell me, I'm not going to like.

"Your brother is here," he informs me, and he was right in being wary of telling me. My hands fist at my sides as I focus on trying not to smash my knuckles into the brand-new mirror. I can't break anything I've set up for her.

"Where is he?" The words are gritted through my clenched teeth. I knew he'd come back to haunt me, but I didn't think he would be so close by.

"Uh… he's working for Mrs. Bardot. She hired him to do the garden, set the fox traps." Gray looks up at me, and I can tell he's more fearful of my wrath than my brother's stupidity. He was around when my brother decided to fuck over the family to join a fucking motorcycle gang. He took the word of murderers instead of his own flesh and blood.

He became someone different. Someone I didn't know, and the more time he spent with his new family, the more he'd forgotten about his lineage. I never forgot, though, and if he thinks he's going to steal *my* payment, he has another thing coming.

"Make sure the girl is safe and stays indoors," I tell Gray. "And if my brother goes near her, I'll kill him myself." I have a feeling my sweet little red isn't someone who'll obey the order to stay indoors. Only, she doesn't know just how feral the predators on the outside are.

"Yes, sir." Gray turns to leave, and I face the mirror once more. I know Darius will do something. I have a feeling the asshole is here to fuck with me. But what he doesn't know is I have ways and means to ensure he can't go near her.

My phone buzzes in my pocket, and when I pull it out to find an unknown number, I'm sure it's my brother. Swiping the screen, I press the device to my ear.

"You know, she's quite the looker," he tells me, the familiar voice ringing in my ears. As much as I hate him, I love him. There's a fine line between the two emotions, a *very* fragile line.

"She's mine, Darius," I inform him, attempting to keep myself calm but failing when my fingers tighten around the cell phone. I only earn myself a chuckle in response.

"And you think the Bardots are just going to let you take her? She's quite curious, isn't she?" He's testing me to see what I'll do, what I'll say. The thing about it is, my brother no longer knows who I am, but I know exactly who he is. I've seen him over the years, had people watching him, and I saw him turn into a monster. My intel has been wrong. He must've known I had eyes on him. The moment I'm done here, I'll have my team fired for fucking this up. They should have known he was in Crimson Falls.

"Darius." His name is a threat on my lips, the tone of my voice giving away just what I'm feeling right this second—pure rage. "I'm not your little brother anymore. I've welcomed the violence that you told me I couldn't find within myself. And as a Shaw, I don't give a shit about family anymore. I will kill you if you go near her."

"From the garden, I can see into her bedroom," he informs me coolly, as if he's telling me about the fucking weather, which certainly doesn't help my anger. My feet carry me out of her room into the hallway. I'm already pulling the gun from my shoulder holster when I reach the ground floor of my house. "She looks so beautiful in her little tank top." His taunts continue with amusement tainting every mumble. My blood boils with every word he utters. "I wonder just how she'd feel squirming under me."

"You'll never find out," I grit, my jaw ticking with feral rage as I pull open my back door and head out into the garden.

"Oh? Perhaps I should lure her outdoors with a pretty flower. And when I do, I'll open her with my blade, just like a blossom being cut from the stem.

Do you think she'll bleed red or blue? I can wait to taste."

"Over my dead body." The words are out of my mouth before I have time to focus on the fact that he's so close by that I can practically smell the violence he emanates. My feet move swiftly across the thick lawn.

What I loved about this property is it connects to the Bardot Manor. Our gardens overlook each other, and I can be on their land in about ten minutes. There is a thick outcropping of trees before reaching it, but I'll get to him, and I'll kill him once and for all.

"Perhaps I'll find out sooner," he tells me. "As you know, curiosity kills the kitten." A scream pierces the speaker before the line dies. *Asshole*. I can't hear anything from where I am, but I quickly make my way down the garden toward the forest that backs up against my property.

I'll find her. I'll find him. And when I do, I'm putting a fucking bullet in his head.

SCARLETT

My throat burns from the scream as I race away from the scary-looking, inked man who stepped out of the shadows. I'm not sure who he is, but I can only guess it's the gardener, the one I was told to stay away from.

"Come on, pretty girl, come out and play," he coos from behind me, his deep voice sending sparks of fear through me, and I push forward, trying to get away from him. "I can smell that sweet fear of yours." His deep voice drips with malice, causing my heart to skitter wildly against my chest.

My long, flowing red hair tangles behind me as thickets and branches snag in my wavy locks. The cool ground beneath my feet causes me to shiver as I race toward the enormous, looming mansion on the other side of the forest.

Footsteps are closing in behind me. I can hear his heavy footfalls, which only have my lungs squeezing, and breathing becomes difficult. I attempt to swallow, but a thick ball of dread threatens to choke me and give me over to the beast behind me.

A howl in the distance forces a squeal of surprise to tumble from my lips. My mother always told me not to go into the woods when I was a kid, but I need to get away from the stranger behind me right now. Another screeching howl comes from somewhere in the darkness, and my heart leaps into my throat.

My lungs burn, and my legs ache.

In, out. In, out.

Breathe, Scarlett.

My heart bangs violently as my lungs slowly start giving out. My breaths are harsh, shallow, and quick. But I push forward, forcing my legs to move quicker, even though I'm ready to pass out. I hit a patch of trees, and then they slowly open as if welcoming me into another world. A house illuminates the darkened world before me with golden light streaming from a few windows.

I'm so close.

The neighbors will help me.

I'm sure they will.

I'm not sure if Estelle or Gray heard me screaming, but someone will figure out I'm gone soon enough. A crack of a branch behind me has another squeal pealing from my lips as I race through the darkness. My skin scrapes and scratches as fearful tears slowly drip from my lashes, making the path blur before me.

I can smell something akin to candle wax, which is strange. And as much as I want to stop, to take a breath because my stomach aches and my chest is tight with exertion, I don't. My feet hit the edge of the forest, and suddenly, I'm ripped backward, my feet flying into the air as strong, thick arms wrap around my waist and haul me back into the gloom of the trees.

"No!" My scream is silenced by a heavy hand covering my mouth, and the more I fight, the tighter the arms hold on to me. My muffled shouts dissipate into the dense trees behind me as I'm dragged through the murkiness.

"If you keep fighting, little red, you'll make my cock hard. I like it when little girls squirm," a deep voice barrels through me, sending ice through my veins, and I still all movement. The man carries me as if I'm weightless, and soon I see a clearing up ahead.

It's not the same voice from earlier, and I wonder who's caught me. The nickname *little red* is what Mr. Shaw called me the night we met at my parent's house, but I know it can't be him. He's not anywhere near Crimson Falls.

The house I saw in the distance becomes clearer, and my captor allows me to my feet, but his hold on me stays strong as his arm snakes around my waist, and when I finally get a glimpse of his face, a gasp tumbles from my mouth.

"What are you doing here?" The shock is clear in my tone, but Mr. Shaw just offers me a sly grin that has dread sluicing through my veins.

"I'm here to keep you safe from the predators out there," he informs me, gesturing with his head toward the forest we just exited. And that's when I take in the house before me. Three floors of pure opulence similar to Gran's mansion, but this one is even bigger, with old brick that looks like it's from a scary movie, rather than modern-day real life.

The windows are lit up, just like I saw from the woods. "Why am I here?"

"Because it's not safe for you to be out there," Mr. Shaw tells me as he leads me into the house via the kitchen door. A similar layout to Gran's with all modern appliances, along with a shiny gas stove that looks like it's never been used.

A table is sprawled along the window, overlooking the garden, and when I glance out toward the property line, I see the dark shadow of my hunter standing there, watching.

"There..." I point, but by the time Shaw looks

out, it's gone. "He was right there." My gaze snaps to his, and I see something flickering in those depths of green. "How did you—"

"Don't ask questions you don't want the answers to," he warns before turning on his heel. I watch him move to the fridge before he pulls open the heavy metal door and asks, "Do you want something to drink?"

"I—I… No, I mean, I need to get home."

"You'll stay here tonight." His tone is no-nonsense as he grabs a bottle of wine and finds a corkscrew in one of the drawers. When he sets two glasses on the breakfast bar, he meets my inquisitive gaze. "I don't want you out there while he's looking for you."

"How do you know he's looking for me?" My curiosity has piqued, and I wonder if Mr. Shaw will offer me the answers I need. I doubt it from the look on his face. He opens the bottle with a pop and pours two generous glasses of white wine before handing me one and taking the other for himself.

"I know things that will cause you to be sick, little red," he tells me. "Now, drink up, and I'll show you to the guest room." My stare is locked on his movements, how he brings the glass to his lips and sips the alcohol. Once again, I'm stunned by just how handsome he is. For someone who was racing through the forest moments ago, he doesn't seem at all perturbed. He hasn't shaved, and like I imagined when we first met, there's a dark dusting of stubble lining his perfectly angular jaw.

"Fine, if you won't tell me how you know, at least tell me your name." I set my glass down, meeting his stare.

His mouth crooks into a wolfish grin as he regards me. "Lycan Shaw," he says, holding out his free hand to mine. "It's lovely to meet you again, Scarlett Bardot."

My gaze falls to his strong hand, and I finally accept it after being at war between wanting to touch him and wanting to run in the opposite direction. We shake, and his thumb circles my skin, sending goose bumps dancing across every inch of me.

"Well, it's a pleasure to meet you too, Lycan." His name tastes like sin on my tongue and poison on my lips. "Why am I here?" I want answers, even though he seems adamant about not giving them to me. But he has to offer an inkling at least.

"Everything will be answered when you get to your room, Scarlett," he informs me before setting his empty glass down and turning for the door. "Follow me."

My mouth gapes then shuts quickly as my feet move behind him, leaving my untouched wine on the counter. "What do you mean, *my* room?"

He doesn't respond. His steps are long strides,

showing off his tall frame and how his slacks and shirt fit him perfectly. There's no doubt this man is breathtakingly gorgeous, but my fight-or-flight instinct has taken over, and I glance at the front door as we pass it.

But Lycan anticipates my thoughts and says, "You can try to run, but there are only two evils you have to deal with, the hunter outside or me." He takes the stairs slowly, waiting for me to make my decision. "But make no mistake, little red," he says, stopping to glance at me from over his shoulder. "I will find you. No matter where you go. The big bad wolf always finds the girl."

The threat is clear. I can't escape, not now. I'm not sure which is worse, being murdered by some crazy person in the forest, or being imprisoned for the evening in a beautiful home with a wolf who seems as lethal as he is beautiful.

When we reach a door on the second floor of the house, Lycan pushes it open and steps aside to allow me to enter the room. It's furnished with a dark wood four-poster bed, an elegantly carved vanity, and two enormous doors that I'm guessing lead to a bathroom and closet.

Spinning on my heel, I take in Lycan as he leans against the doorframe. His shoulders relaxed, arms folded, as he focuses on me. Those deep, luminous, green depths expose my fear as he stares at me from top to bottom and up again.

I ask once more, "Why am I here?"

LYCAN

Her gaze is burning as she regards me, perusing every inch of me. Those full lips purse into a pout, frustrated at not knowing what's happening. It's evident that she's angry, and I smile.

"What the fuck is going on?" Her arms cross over her chest, causing her tits to perk up as she storms toward me. I expect her to touch me, punch me, or slap me, but she doesn't. And I find that I *want* her to put her hands on me.

She's close—inches from where I'm leaning against the doorframe to her bedroom. The scent of her perfume invades my nostrils, and it takes over my senses as she pins her glare on mine. Her lips purse as her nose scrunches.

"If you don't tell me—"

Tipping my head to the side, I narrow my gaze on hers. "What? You'll what?" The challenge in my tone is clear. I quirk my lips at the corner, a smile ready to dance along my mouth as I focus on her.

"I don't know," she backs down. "I just need to know why I'm here, what you want with me, and who that man was chasing me. You clearly know him since you were there to *save* me."

"That's a lot of information for a little girl to take in. Isn't it?" My brow lifts at her in question, and the blaze of her stare sizzles as she narrows her eyes.

"I'm not a little girl. I'm a woman. And I need to know what's going on. Or I'll walk home." In her attempt to walk past me, my hand shoots out, gripping her wrist, tugging it closer to me. "Let me go, Lycan."

I want nothing more than to pin her down and spank her ass until she's begging for mercy, I will not show. Keeping my voice calm, I command, "You'll stay here, Scarlett."

"No. I don't want to." She sounds like a petulant teenager, but I can't deny her voice is like an aphrodisiac to me.

Chuckling, I push off the doorframe and grip both her shoulders, lifting her off her feet. I walk toward the bed dumping her on the mattress, causing her to bounce on the softness of the bed. "Stay." When I turn, I expect her next move as she tries to make her escape, but I'm fast, much faster than her.

My arms wrap around her, bringing her back to the bed and pushing her onto her back. Her legs and arms attempt to attack me, but she's not strong enough, and seconds later, I have her wrists bound to the wooden poles of the headboard and her ankles tied to the foot end.

"What the fuck are you doing?" Her rage bounces off the walls. The poison she shoots at me from her gaze should hurt, but I closed myself off to emotions a long time ago. There are instances in my life I allow myself to feel, and that's when I'm dominating a woman in a scene.

Other than that, I'm cold, heartless, and unfeeling.

"Let me go!"

"Your screaming won't earn you your freedom," I tell her, keeping my tone calm, neutral, which only has her tugging at the restraints that will never let her loose. I've bound her too tight, and the sight of her lying there, ready for me, has an effect I knew to expect.

Her vulnerability in this moment has my cock throbbing against my zipper.

I'd love nothing more than to strip her bare and feast on her, but I have things to do. I have a brother to kill.

"Please," she pleads, her voice turning soft, but the heat in her eyes still dances with a threat of death if she were to wield a weapon. Thankfully, it doesn't faze me. If I were stupid, if I were years younger, I would've wilted for her, but I'm no longer weak.

"You'll stay. Once I'm done with my business, I'll return for you." I make my way to the door. Twisting the handle, I tug it open and step out into the hallway to her screams. Once I shut her inside, her voice gets muffled by the thick wood.

Leaning my head against the cool surface, I close my eyes and listen to her for a while longer before I lock her in and head down to my study. I promised Kahn he would be able to go to the church to seek out the priest who may have news about his sister, but I need him and his team here.

My brother has gone rogue, and I'm done playing games. Picking up my cell phone, I hit dial on Kahn's number. Four rings and he finally answers—out of breath and gravelly.

"Are you busy fucking?" I ask my tone taking on a gruff rumble.

Kahn chuckles. "No, Mr. Shaw, I was working out. Late night in the gym," he tells me. "What can I do for you?"

"Are you leaving for the convent soon? Or are you still in New York?" I settle back in the expensive leather chair and close my eyes. My head is pounding from today's shitshow, and even with Scarlett upstairs, safe, I'm not at ease. If Darius is so adamant about stealing her, he could walk in here at any moment. Not that I won't see him approach, but the thought of a fight tonight doesn't bode well for the state I'm in.

"I'm still around. Did you need me?"

"I'll make sure the jet is ready when you get to the airstrip. I need you in Crimson Falls before sunrise," I inform him. "Bring the team. I have a feeling this could be a tough job."

"What's happening?" Usually, I wouldn't tell the men until they were all in the room with me, but this is a special case. I've never asked them to do something so personal before. Killing my brother is not something I planned to do for a while yet, but when someone threatens my life, livelihood, and possessions, I fight back.

"Darius is here, and he needs to be taken care of as soon as possible."

Silence greets me. I'm certain Kahn is in shock at my response. If I had to be honest, I am too. Holding someone's life in your hands is a powerful feeling. Something that takes hold and doesn't let go. Not easily anyway.

"I'll make sure the guys are on the flight."

"Thank you." I hang up before tapping out a message to the pilot. Once my men get here, we can map out a plan. There's a lot to do with only a week to go before the ball and at least a month before my marriage to Scarlett. Especially getting her ready and onboard.

That's going to be my toughest challenge yet.

SCARLETT

When I open my eyes, I shoot up from the comfortable, form-hugging mattress to find I'm no longer bound. Instinctively, I glance at my wrists to find a hint of the bindings that kept me prisoner. I'm not sure how much time has passed. I must've been exhausted that I fell asleep while bound to the goddamned bed.

Lycan Shaw is a monster, but I need answers. I push off the bed, feeling the softness of the carpet underfoot, and for a moment, my toes dig into the thick wool. The curtains hang open, and I notice it's still dark out. Surely the sun is coming up soon.

Pacing the room, I stop when I hear a sound outside in the garden a story down, and I notice Lycan stalking from the house toward the property line. The shadow I saw earlier is gone, but it doesn't make sense that he's out there when he didn't want me going home. I wonder if the staff knows I'm missing, or if Gran has called the house and they've informed her I'm not there.

I didn't see Estelle or Gray when I walked out last night. They must know I'm no longer in the house. The staff must've heard me scream. Surely, they'll come to find me.

A shot rings in the air, causing me to jump back from the window. I suck in a shocked breath and hold it, listening for more volatile sounds, but silence greets me. I exhale and find my lungs struggle to pull in more air as my heart thumps at my ribs.

I should've run when I could, when he released me, but there's something about Lycan Shaw that intrigues me. *Why would he save me and then keep me prisoner?*

I turn back to the bed to find something lying on the nightstand I didn't see earlier. Lycan's earlier words ring in my mind as I pick up the creamy, thick paper folded into a rectangle. *"Everything will be answered when you get to your room."* Ripping open the envelope, I pull out the letter that's been folded three times over. The handwriting is familiar, and I recognize it instantly. It's my father's scrawl, signed at the bottom of what looks like a contract.

I scan the pages of the terms and conditions. Every word, each sentence, sends ice through my veins. My father signed my life, my hand in marriage, over to Lycan Shaw. There's no reasoning behind it, just that he thinks it's better for me in the long run. The words *safe and secure* are underlined a few times in thick black ink.

I read it and reread it, but nothing makes sense.

Dad wants me to marry a man who's possibly twice my age. Someone I have only ever met once at dinner a few nights ago—a man who stole me from the forest and brought me to a gilded prison.

When I glance up at the room once more, I take in each detail, every corner, each item. Every inch of this bedroom has been created especially for me, from the mirror with the carving of Little Red Riding Hood and the wolf, to the bedding that is in my favorite color.

The door flies open, and standing on the threshold is the man who *bought* me from my father. His expression is calm, but his tense posture has the hair on the back of my neck prickling.

"What is this?" I ask him, throwing the contract onto the bed before making my way toward him. Anger surges through me as his mouth tips slightly. "I asked you a fucking question, Mr. Shaw," I mutter, spitting his name with as much venom as I can conjure. "I'm not a fucking possession you can barter with like that. I'm a woman, a *person*. What kind of man buys a woman from her father?"

He doesn't react; he merely watches me, intrigue dancing in his gaze. His nonreaction only sends my rage into a spiral. My gut twists as he regards me with cold indifference, the smirk on his handsome face turning upward.

"Talk to me!" My fists pound against his chest, but I only get one hit in before his hands grip my wrists. A deep rumble vibrates through his chest as he pushes me back until my ass hits the edge of the mattress.

Lycan leans in, his tall frame cocooning me as he stops inches from where I'm bending backward painfully. I know if I were to lean back further, I'd end up pinned between him and the mattress where I slept last night, my hands still in his hold as he pushes them to my sides. He takes this opportunity to kick my feet apart before stepping in between my legs, causing me to tumble onto the soft comforter. The hardness of his desire presses against my core, forcing heat to sizzle between my legs at the contact.

"If you ever lift your hands at me again," he speaks, calm, clear, and threatening, "I will bend you over and whip you with my belt until you're bleeding all over my pristine carpets. Am I understood?"

There's not a hint of anger in his voice, but his eyes, they're expressive, burning like open flames as they pierce me. The depths steal me into their darkness the closer he gets. His lips brush along mine, and as angry as I am at him, I can't deny my body trembles under his.

The power he exudes sends heat blazing to my cheeks, and my stomach tumbles and twists with a need for him to move, for him to press harder against my center.

What the fuck is wrong with you, Scarlett?

I hiss when he tightens his hold on my wrists, the harshness of his fingers pressing hard against my smooth skin, and I'm sure there'll be bruises, not from the bindings, but from his touch.

"Get the fuck off me." My words are meant to sting, but instead, Lycan chuckles at my outburst. "I'm serious." He doesn't move, and even though my rage is burning a blaze through me, I can't stop my body from responding to him.

"So am I." There is no doubt in my mind that he will whip me, and he will enjoy every moment of my torture. He pushes away from me, and an unwarranted whimper of agony escapes my lips. "Are you hungry?"

"What?" The query pops out of my mouth with shock drenching the word. My mouth gapes at him, my eyes wide, confusion settling in my chest.

"I don't like repeating myself," he throws back easily, his grin making him seem younger than what

I can only guess is about forty years.

"No. I'm not. I want answers." I don't want to sound like a petulant child, but I know I do. I can hear it in my voice. It annoys me that he does this to me. I'm not *this* girl. One who acts like an immature teenager, but something about Lycan Shaw makes me feel young.

Lycan stays silent for a long while before he sighs. "Your father fucked up," he speaks, turning his back on me as he moves to the vanity. His fingers trail over the smooth surface before he glances at the window as if seeing something in the murkiness outside. "He did things that were…" He pauses for a long moment, and my mind whirs with something Dad would've done, and I want to scream. "Illegal." He doesn't look at me as he tells me this, and I wonder what my father could've done that was so bad. He's always been a good man. At least to me, he's been a good father. "He has secrets only I know, and that's why he'll repay me with your hand."

"I don't understand. Why not arrest him?" I push to my feet, needing to stand for this, or at least I think I need to be. "Lycan?" Lycan's steps fall softly on the carpet as he takes two strides toward the window while keeping his back to me. For a moment, he stands there silently, and I wonder if he'll answer.

His hand threads through his dark hair, a lock

falling into a shimmering eye as he gazes at me over his shoulder. "Your father is a smart man, but I'm smarter. He wanted more than he could hold onto, including your mother. He thought secrets would remain hidden forever, but he fucked with the wrong person."

My curiosity wins out as he trickles information to me, and I lap it up like a puppy needing sustenance. I take a couple of tentative steps toward him. "What do you mean?"

"He stole from me," Lycan says, his profile half shadowed as he regards the window, his focus on the outside instead of me. "And now I've taken from him." That's when he turns to look at me. His one hand landing on the edge of the wooden vanity, his knuckles turning white, and I wonder briefly if he's reigning in his desire to be near me.

"You can't *steal* me. This isn't some archaic eye for an eye belief," I bite out, forgetting that this man holds all the power. But then again, I have control as well. He can't do anything to me if I don't want him to. He wouldn't force me. He can't.

"Those questions racing through your pretty little head right now, they're pointless," he tells me in his smooth baritone, a hint of an accent brightening his words, making them seem lyrical. "Because I can do anything I want, to anyone I want, at any time I want." This time, he turns toward me fully, showing off his height, broadness, and dominance. The control and power that follow him like perfume grip my chest squeeze the breath from my lungs, and I can't find the response I need and crave.

"Don't treat me like a child."

He chuckles before stepping away from the soft, silver illumination streaming into the bedroom from the moon outside. "Then don't act like one," Lycan counters seriously. He leans against the vanity, and for a moment, I see him as the wolf, but something internally, my gut, tells me he's not. "I'm not the bad guy here."

"You *bought* me from my father. I think that makes you the asshole."

"If you continue to curse like that, I'm going to be forced to take you under hand and show you how naughty girls are treated," he bites out, those jade orbs flaring with danger as he pins me in place with a stare.

"Oh?" I challenge. "What? Are you going to spank me, *asshole*?" I have no clue what I'm doing, why I'm taunting him like this, but a second later, before I have time to apologize, his body is looming over me, his one hand gripping both of mine as he spins us around, shoving me against the smooth wooden surface he was just leaning against. My butt sticks out toward him, which only makes me blush. Thankfully, I'm still wearing shorts, and I'm not naked in front of a man who *bought* me.

His hand comes down in a loud, harsh swat against one cheek of my bottom, and then the other. Alternating between the two, he spanks me hard, painfully, causing the sting to trickle its way over my skin.

Embarrassment floods my mind.

My cheeks hot and red, and my panties... those are soaked from the assault.

LYCAN

Her body trembles under my hold. The gentle curves of her frame have my erection thickening with the need to slide into her heat. To hear her cry out. Soft whimpers free themselves from her pouted lips, and I can't help but smile at her. Our reflection in the mirror shows my dominance, but it's her submission in this moment that has my cock rock-hard.

"Are you going to act like a petulant child, or can I release you now?" I ask, trailing my fingertips over her spine, reveling in her reaction to me. A moan of deep pleasure escapes her when I reach the juncture between her thighs. Heat spills easily from the apex of her figure as I taunt her pussy over the thin layers of the soft, cotton shorts that hide what

87

I crave.

"Please," Scarlett pleads, but I'm not sure what she's asking for. More of the same or for me to release her from my hold. "Please, Lycan."

Leaning in, I engulf her with my body, keeping her in place, allowing my lips to trail over the shell of her ear before I ask, "What, little red? Tell me what this pretty pussy craves." The command is gentle, a caress of words along her smooth, porcelain flesh.

"I... I can't marry you," she whimpers as my finger continues to taunt her. "I—I don't want to be arm candy for an asshole who doesn't love me." A tear slips free from her long lashes, and as it trickles down her flushed cheek, I lap it up, tasting the salty emotion as it spills from her eyes.

"You're not arm candy," I tell her because it's the truth. She's so much more than that. "If you think for one moment I'm going to let you go, to walk out of my life..." I inhale a deep breath to keep calm. "Then you're sorely mistaken. You are mine. I own you now, and you will submit to me. Perhaps not tonight, but soon." I press down on her clit, sending her over the edge, and her keening cry is music to my ears.

I watch her ride the wave of her release for a long while before I step back, finally releasing her from the confines of my body. Scarlett straightens, her glassy eyes flicking to mine. Heat, confusion, and a hint of anger swirl in her gaze. But the shame that colors her cheeks has me wanting to see more of it in her expression.

"Why did you do that?" Her words are croaky, her body still shivering from the intensity of what just happened. My cock, on the other hand, feels like steel against my zipper. "Why?"

"Because I like to make pretty girls cry," I respond. "And because you are mine. My little red. And nobody is going to take you away from me."

She straightens her shoulders, tilting her chin in challenge as her eyes narrow. "What if I want to walk away from you?"

"Learn about your father's transgressions before you make your choice. There are always a lesser of two evils in this world." I shrug, shoving my hands in my pockets before I continue. "And your choice should come from knowing all the information."

"Then tell me," she pleads, tears filling her lashes, threatening to fall. She looks so beautiful on the verge of breaking down, and I want so badly to pin her to the wooden vanity and claim her, mark her as mine.

"Give me a week," I request. "Should you feel the need to leave after, I'll rethink the terms of the contract."

Her eyes widen farther, those glossy orbs holding me hostage, and for a moment, I allow her to ponder what I've just said. Then she mouths, "A whole week?"

Nodding slowly, I focus on keeping my expression calm, collected, and not allowing the desire that's burning its way through every inch of my body to show. She doesn't need to know I'm on the verge of fucking her until she's screaming the roof down. "While you're in my house, you will not touch yourself. Every orgasm you have while you're here, and trust me, there will be many, are mine to give you. I own you, Scarlett; it's written on that contract."

"You can't own someone. If I'm not willing to give you something, you can't take it," she sasses, crossing her arms, but I don't miss the tremble in her hands.

A smirk curls my lips, and I raise a dark brow at her in a challenge. If she thinks I'm a good man who won't take what I want, then she's mistaken.

"Right? You wouldn't…" Her words filter into nothing, the silence deafening when she realizes I'm no gentleman.

Taking a step toward her, I notice her attempt at moving away, but she's now pinned between me and the smooth wood of the vanity. She's small, only reaching my chest, so she has to tip her head back to look me in the eye.

There's a hint of fear, but it's mingled with

curiosity. When I close the distance between my mouth and hers, I notice desire dancing in her eyes, but the moment she blinks, it's gone.

"Don't underestimate me." I keep my voice calm. My composure is hanging by a thread when her tongue darts out, wetting her plump lips. "When I sign a contract, when I agree to anything, I don't break that promise. You will say your vows in a month, and when you sign your name, it will be Shaw, not Bardot. On your twenty-first birthday, you will be my wife."

Another emotion dances across her expression before she asks, "And if I refuse?"

"There is no choice in the matter. Whatever you do, wherever you go, you are mine. And I take care of my belongings. Now, I want you to sleep. When the sun has risen on this day, we'll talk more." I step back, needing the space because I'm so close to ripping her clothes off and seeing what I now own. Turning on my heel, I make it to the door before I hear a soft whimper. She's crying, but tears don't afford her mercy. They only make my dick hard.

"Will I ever see my family again?" Her question has me stalling, the door ajar, and my one foot over the threshold. When I glance over my shoulder, I see her, the girl under the strong façade she tries to portray, and it only makes me want her more.

"We'll talk in the morning." I shut the door

behind me, knowing that if I were to have stayed in that room for a moment longer, I would've taken everything that belongs to me. Twisting the golden key in the lock, I leave her to mull over her situation.

I have things to do.

A brother to kill.

And a priest to call.

SCARLETT

I spent the night tossing and turning. Dreams of a big bad wolf invaded my mind and took hold of me. All I saw behind my lids was a large predator following me through the woods as I tried to get home.

At one point, I actually believed I was out in the cold with the enormous gray wolf following me, but when my eyes snap open in shock, I shiver but find myself alone in the immaculate room that Lycan confirmed is mine.

The rising sun is slowly brightening the deep purple sky beyond the curtains, which in turn illuminates my bedroom. I have to be honest; the bed was comfortable even though I didn't get a lot of sleep. I'm sure I would have had a great evening if I wasn't being kept captive in a mansion owned by the man who's convinced he's going to marry me.

My mind still cannot fathom how my father could have signed over my life to someone like this. *Did he know Lycan long before he agreed to this preposterous contract?* I wonder how long the two men who clearly want to rule my life knew each other before Lycan requested this bullshit. I'm not marrying him. And he doesn't realize how much I'll fight back, because if he thinks otherwise, he is misleading himself.

I need to talk to my dad or even my mother because the idea of being with a man like Lycan Shaw forever doesn't leave me all warm and fuzzy. But then the memory of what he did to me last night assaults every sense. My skin prickles as the phantom touch of him teases me. I can't stop the ache that slowly tightens in my stomach when I recall how his fingers brought me pleasure, even as anger rolled through me.

He's an expert.

He clearly knows my body and can manipulate me like a musical instrument, but that's only an indication of how many women he's been with, and that's not a man I want to spend my life with. When I do decide to give myself to someone, to take their name, it will be because I'm the only one they're with. I don't share, and I certainly will not be a wife forced to bear children while he goes fucking everything in a skirt.

When the bedroom door opens again, I'm met with a gentle smile from an older woman I haven't seen before. She moves into the room and sets down a tray that has a plate covered with a silver dome, along with coffee, which I can smell from my bed, and a glass of orange juice.

"Mr. Shaw will be with you soon," she says before heading out, leaving me alone to ponder just what *Mr. Shaw* wants to do today. Perhaps he'd like to kick a puppy. Rolling my eyes at the childish thought, I push off the bed and make my way to the tray. I reach for the coffee first, which is rich and dark, and I add a splash of milk from a small porcelain jug and a spoon of sugar, which I slowly stir into the liquid.

"Didn't take you for having a sweet tooth." His deep baritone comes from behind me, and I almost drop the mug, but I set it down before I face him. I take him in, allowing my gaze to rove over him from head to toe. Dressed casually in a pair of dark blue jeans and a Henley, which matches the color of emeralds, I can't help but admire just how handsome he is.

His tanned skin, with the dark dusting of stubble now closer to being a beard than not, makes my thighs involuntarily squeeze together. He doesn't come inside; he lurks on the threshold of the bedroom, and I wonder if he's staying far from me to hold onto some form of restraint.

"What was that gunshot last night?" I ask, remembering seeing him in the darkness, hearing the loud echo ringing in my ears. His expression turns dark as if he's shutting down the hatches, keeping all the secrets inside. Those emeralds simmer with rage for a split second, but with a blink, it's gone.

I expect an answer, but when he opens his mouth, he changes the topic. "The priest will be here this evening to meet with us. I want us to write our own vows," he says nonchalantly as he crosses his arms and leans against the wall not far from the door.

He knows what he's doing. Keeping the escape route blocked. Even if I could get past his looming frame, I have a feeling I wouldn't get very far. He'll catch me without putting in any effort.

"You want me to write vows?" Incredulity laces my tone, causing Lycan to chuckle. "I'm not marrying you." I'm adamant, squaring my shoulders after stepping away from the vanity, leaving my coffee behind. I'm almost certain I'm going to need two hands for this interaction.

"Of course you are," he says. "It's in the contract. You have no choice in this, Scarlett." He straightens, pushing his hands into his pockets, forcing my attention to drop to his crotch, which has my stomach fluttering wildly at the thought of what he's hiding in there.

Snapping my eyes to his, I shake my head. "No. What you're suggesting is archaic, just something my parents would do to piss me off. To rule my life as if I were still a child."

"Oh?" His dark brows arch as he watches me inquisitively. "If you force my hand, Scarlett, I will happily bind you to me and carry you down that fucking aisle." His tone is a crash of no-nonsense whiplash—commanding and domineering.

"And what? You expect me to wear a pretty white dress as well?" My sneer is evident.

His smirk is unmistakable. "Let me make something clear," Lycan says, taking two long strides closer to me, eating up the distance before he continues. "You will be Mrs. Shaw by the time this month is over. On your birthday, you will be mine." And that's when it hits me — I turn twenty-one in a few weeks, and he wants us to exchange our vows. I never once thought I'd be married so young.

Narrowing my gaze, I tip my head to the side as I watch his reaction to my next question. "What do you want? Why me?"

This time, he moves closer, swallowing the inches that keep us apart, wedging me between his muscled thighs and the furniture. "I want a queen, little red," he speaks softly, his voice merely a taunting whisper as his breath wafts warmly over me. "I want a woman I can proudly walk beside in public. To watch every man's eyes on her while they slobber for a chance to take her, but knowing she is mine. In her elegant beauty, she'll shine amongst the fake, plastic smiles while I introduce her to my world."

He stays silent for a moment, probably waiting for what he just said to sink in. When he doesn't continue, I prompt, "What else?"

"I also want that same woman to come home with me every evening and allow me to fuck her until she can't think straight. I want to wear her out, make her cry and scream, make her come, and then I want her to take my seed. I want her porcelain flesh to be marred by my mark. The bruises I'll bestow on her skin will be my ownership of her, and when my cock isn't inside her, she'll feel the emptiness. The craving to have me will be her addiction, and her heart will be my ultimate prize."

My heart catapults into my throat at the elicit promise of what he wants and needs from me. And deep down, I wonder if I can give that to him. I'm not some sweet, submissive doll he can dress and play with. Folding my arms in front of me, I meet those deep, jade depths. "You want arm candy and a fuck toy." I shake my head as realization takes hold of me, and the picture becomes clear.

"If you want to put it so callously." He shrugs before a small, wolfish grin tilts his perfectly pink mouth. "But..." Lycan reaches for my hair, tangling a lock of my long, red strands around his finger before tugging. The smaller smile from seconds ago turns dangerous as the corners of his mouth tilt upward, and he continues, "I want someone with intelligence who can stand beside me while running my business. A woman with strength and fire."

My mouth falls open, gaping at his admission. I never expected him to give me so much honesty. "And that's why you chose me?"

"Oh, little red, no." He shakes his head. A somewhat hungry stare burns through me as he offers me a slight chuckle. His tongue teases his lower lip before his perfectly pearly whites bite down on the flesh, forcing my eyes to lock on the full, pinkish mouth I'm tempted to taste. "I was given you as a payment. I didn't know I would *want* you until the night we met."

"That makes no sense."

He tugs my hair once more before gripping my chin between his thumb and forefinger. "When you spoke back to me, when that fire burned in your eyes, that's when I decided I'll take you, and your father agreed." A flash of satisfaction dances in his darkening gaze before he leans in, his mouth teasing its way over my cheek to my ear. "And that makes you mine."

The heat of his breath and the promise in his tone has my skin bursting with goose bumps, the tightening in my gut twisting with a need for more pain as he tugs at my hair. My thighs instinctively squeeze together even though I try to fight the desire that's burning through every inch of me. My stomach somersaults with a flurry of nerves when Lycan's teeth graze the supple flesh of my ear lobe.

I don't know what I'm supposed to do here.

I want to hate Lycan, and I think I do, but also, anger at my parents takes precedence.

But even under all that, there's the need for him that's coursing through my veins like a drug. It's as if I've been shot up with something strong and volatile, something I'm not sure I can fight. Even though I know, I should.

Pulling away, I lock my glare on him before I voice, "I won't marry you." But the hoarsely whispered words aren't as strong as they were earlier.

"We'll see," Lycan responds before stepping back, leaving me cold and shivering at his absence. "Eat. Enjoy your coffee. I'll see you later." He heads to the door and stops on the threshold, glancing at me from over his shoulder before winking.

And then he's gone, and I'm left angry and frustrated.

SCARLETT

Unconvinced.

That's the emotion coursing through me when I wake up in the darkened bedroom. When I think about marrying Lycan, I'm unsure of myself, of his intentions, which he seemed to make clear last night, but there's a hint of doubt plaguing me.

Pushing off the bed, I pad barefoot to the window, pulling open the heavy, lined curtains to find what looks like a chilly morning, the grass shimmering with drops of dew settled on the green blades. The forest beyond seems to swallow up the light, offering only a warning—don't enter here.

I move to the vanity, taking in the beautifully carved wood, the smooth surface where Lycan had pinned me down before spanking my ass. The memory is still fresh in my mind, replaying when I need it least. I don't want to remember how his hands felt on me, but every interaction so far has been intense. And if I had to be honest, it's left me frustrated—more at the fact that he has such an effect on me.

I shouldn't *want* him, but my body betrays me each time. The man is an Adonis, and when he's around me, I'm merely a mortal girl, one with needs that flare like wildfire at his touch. Shaking my head, I go into the bathroom to freshen up before dressing in a pair of leggings, and a large sweater that falls just below my butt. Slipping on a pair of ballet flats, I pull my hair into a messy bun before I open my bedroom door.

He hasn't given me an order not to explore the house. Instead of sitting in the room, I'm going to try to learn more about the man who's stolen me. If I can find a phone, perhaps I can call my grandmother. She'll know what to do.

At the thought of her, I wonder if she knows Lycan. Surely, being neighbors, she would need to know the person living next door to her. The fact that he knows my father is also jarring. A connection that is still confusing me. Growing up, I never heard the Shaw or even about Lycan himself. *Why has he only now appeared in my life?*

My feet carry me down the long hallway, silently over the carpets which line the floor, leading me from door to door. Each one I push open is another bedroom. By the time I reach the far end, the last door is locked, and I can't for the life of me figure out if it's another bedroom or if on the other side is something far more sinister.

A giggle bubbles in my chest at the thought. I've been reading far too many romance novels. My mind is clearly playing tricks on me. But I wouldn't put it past Lycan to have a *red room* where he would torture women into submission.

Heat sizzles over my skin, leaving goosebumps in the wake of the thoughts that take hold of me. *I don't want Lycan.* And even as I tell myself silently that it's true, my mind and body are at war.

Ignoring the niggling at what's behind the black, wooden door, I turn and head for the staircase, leading me down to the ground floor. The house is silent. There's not even a clink of cutlery or crockery from the kitchen.

The smooth, marble tiles muffle my steps as I head into the living room to find it empty. The house is immaculate with furnishings that ooze wealth and beauty, something I've grown up with, and so I'm accustomed to the stench of money. It reeks. As thankful as I am that I didn't have to get a student loan for my studies, I also know just how much responsibility comes from having family money.

I wonder briefly about Lycan. He's much older than I am, but I'm sure he must feel some heaviness from always having to be flawless. When you're thrown into social circles all your life, it comes with the expectation that you're perfect. But nobody can be, and that's something my mother never understood.

Every inch of the house has been decorated with the utmost care, from the color of the fabrics to the paint against the walls. The floor underfoot is warm, and I wonder if there's a heating system hidden from sight.

"Oh," a soft voice of shock comes from behind me, causing me to spin on my heel. A woman, who looks to be about my age, stands before me, a silver tray in hand.

"Hello."

"Hi," she greets. Her eyes are wide, her mouth tilting upwards at the corners. "Are you...?" Her voice falters, her cheeks turning a soft pink as she regards me. "Are you here for Mr. Shaw?" The way she's looking at me makes me feel as if she's assessing me.

"I..." Honestly, I have no clue how to answer her. *Am I here for him? Or am I a prisoner in his house?* A bit of both. I'm not sure why Lycan wants me of all people. Surely there are a million women out there who would be better suited to him. "I'm not sure," I finally tell her.

"Oh," she whispers, setting the tray down gently. She moves quietly as she places the cup, small teapot, and plate on the setting at the head of a long, wooden dining table. The silver cutlery shimmers as the sunlight that's now streaming through the patio doors brighten the space. Once she's readied everything, she steps away.

"What is your name?"

The young woman glances at me with uncertainty on her pretty features. With chestnut hair tied into a ponytail at the back of her head and porcelain features, I wonder if Lycan finds her attractive.

Shaking my head to clear the stupidly jealous thoughts away, I focus on her. "I'm Scarlett. My family lives next door. Well, my grandmother does."

"You're the Bardot?" Her gasp is loud, her eyes even wider than before, the blue tinkling like sparkles in the sunlight. "I... I didn't realize you'd be here."

Confusion settles in my gut, my brows furrowed before I ask, "What do you mean?"

Her mouth opens as if to respond, but a moment later, she shakes her head and makes to leave me alone in the room with more questions than I have answers.

"Wait, please. I didn't mean to upset you."

She glances at me from over her shoulder, her expression void of emotion as she looks at me. "My name is Aliana," she tells me. "Please, don't ever speak to me again. It's best that way." Before I can ask something more, she's gone. The door to where I'm guessing the kitchen is hidden swings shut, and I'm alone.

What have I done to her to make her so angry?

The door I entered through opens, and there on the threshold is the man who brought me here. Dressed in a gray suit and black button-up, he looks like he's ready for board meetings, and I wonder what work he does. I don't recall him telling me, and I don't remember if my father mentioned it at the dinner when we first met.

"Now, this is a sight I could get used to every morning," Lycan says with a wolfish smirk, making his handsome face light up with amusement. "What are you doing here, little red?" He moves through the room as if floating on air. When he finally reaches me, I take in the dark stubble on his jaw, and for a moment, my hand tingles with the need to touch it.

"I... I was just exploring the house and found my way in here," I tell him, omitting the fact that I met Aliana. The pretty girl seemed to not want me around, and to be completely honest, I wouldn't want to be around here, but I know if I tried to leave, Lycan would find me before I made it next door.

"Well, sit," he tells me before pulling out one of the chairs, which I slide into. Perhaps Lycan will give me answers. I can only hope and pray. "I'll call your grandmother later," he informs me, which has me straightening my back.

"Let me talk to her. I need to understand—"

"You don't need to do anything." His dark green gaze lands on me, holding me hostage, stealing the breath from my lungs with the dark promise of something I truly don't want to fathom. He is danger wrapped up in a tailored suit. That's all it is. Undeniably handsome, but also unpredictable in his demeanor.

"I need to speak to my family. You cannot hold me here for no reason. I'm not your property, even though my father signed that godforsaken agreement." My voice is brittle with frustration, my throat feels dry as if sandpaper has lodged itself in my esophagus, and with each word I utter, it only seems to hurt more and more.

"If you'd like to talk to someone, it can be your friend, Aelin. Other than that, you're not to talk to anyone else." His voice comes out with a warning that if I were to try anything, he'd know, and he would hurt me.

"Then let me speak to her," I plead because if I can talk to her, then she can get help. She can call my father and get him to sort this mess out. Fix what he did.

Lycan ignores me for a moment as he pours the hot tea into a cup. I watch as he drops a small spoon of sugar into the liquid and stirs a few times. Once he sets the teaspoon down, he shoves the cup toward me. "Drink this. It will calm that fire so we can talk like adults."

"Don't treat me—"

"Scarlett," he growls, my name a warning on his lips, his eyes blazing with fury when he looks at me again. "If you don't want to obey me, I'll happily tie you to the St Andrew's cross in my dungeon and leave you there, naked and crying, until you realize I'm the one in charge here."

My mouth falls open in shock, but my body responds to his threat with heat sizzling in my veins. The apex of my thighs pulsing with unrelenting need, and I can't stop myself from squirming in the seat. I don't want him to have this hold over me, this effect that sends me rabid with hunger for him to do just what he's promising. But I can't help it. My traitorous desires take hold when Lycan throws his dark promises at me.

"You may be in charge in this house, but you don't own me."

"Yet," he adds, knowing he has me because my father has agreed to allow Lycan to marry me. "Are you joining me for breakfast, or are you going to your room to sit alone?" Lycan asks so gently I snap my gaze to his, finding in those emerald orbs genuine concern.

"Do you want me to eat with you?" I'm not sure why, but after I voice my query, my heart gallops like a wild horse in a field, enjoying its freedom. But it won't last long because that stupid muscle that beats wants him to say yes. Even though my mind is convinced he must say no, that I should *want* him to say no. I don't.

For a long moment, Lycan watches me, taking in my hair, my face. When his gaze lands on my mouth, his tongue darts out to wet his full lips. "Yes, stay. Perhaps you'll enjoy my company and realize I'm not as bad as you think," he tells me as a satisfied grin forms on his perfectly handsome face.

"I doubt that," I bite out, taunting the wolf while sitting in his den. I must be stupid, but this man brings out the childlike qualities I've always had. "What could you possibly tell me to make me change my mind about marrying you?"

"Besides the fact that I saved your life... That would be my brother. And he isn't a man you want to be caught in the dark with. He's a hunter. He enjoys making pretty girls his toys."

My eyes widen in surprise at his confession, but quickly recover before testing, "Just like you?" I realize he could get angry. He could lock me in my room and never let me out, but I can't find it in myself to sit quietly.

"The women I take are willing accomplices to the pleasures I bestow on their bodies. I didn't hear you complaining while you drenched my fingers." Lycan picks up his mug, sipping his coffee as he regards me.

The door behind us opens, and the girl from earlier appears once more, this time with two plates of breakfast, including a mound of delicious-looking scrambled eggs, two rashers of bacon, and what I can only guess is dark rye toast.

Once we're alone, I look at Lycan before speaking. "I'm a woman. A touch from someone handsome, someone who's just saved my life is—"

"That's bullshit, and you know it," Lycan throws back. "You like the danger," he tells me with the confidence of someone who's known me all my life. "There are women out there who crave it, who ache for the need to be taken, owned, to be submissive under a man who knows how to make them feel something."

"I feel—"

My throat constricts when his eyes land on me, and I can't find words because I've never seen such unadulterated desire like I find in Lycan's stare. He leans back, his fork dropping on his plate with a loud clatter that echoes in the silence hanging heavily in the room around us.

"Look me in the eye. Tell me honestly that you don't enjoy the feeling of being helpless," he requests with a dark undertone to his voice, one that's gritted in gravel and drenched in desire.

My mouth opens to retort some form of denial, something to tell Lycan Shaw he's wrong about me, but I can't. Not because I'm scared, but because he's right. My stomach twists with the memory of what he did to me, how he touched me while holding me down on the cool surface of the vanity. And every moment of that only confirmed what I already knew—I'm broken.

"You don't have to be ashamed," he says before forking eggs into his mouth. His jaw works as he chews, and it's the sexiest thing I've ever seen. His chiseled face has the makings of a perfect sculpture, and I wonder just how many women have fallen prey to the man who's sitting at the head of the long table.

"I'm not ashamed about anything," I tell him. "There are things that aren't spoken about in my friend circles. In the society I grew up in, sex was something that happened behind closed doors." It's true. There weren't any women who opened up about their personal lives. There were no confessions about husbands and boyfriends who were good or bad in bed and certainly no conversations about their own pleasure.

Even my best friend, as open-minded as she is, is not one for oversharing. Sometimes that's a good thing, but other times, it's lonely. Not to have anyone to confide in. So, I kept my secrets to myself.

"That's the trouble with the old money society," Lycan says as he breaks through my thoughts. "They're far too conservative, only to do the darkest, dirtiest things in secret." A glint of knowing sparkles in his gem-like eyes.

"Oh?" I want to know. Curiosity has always been my downfall, and right now, I want Lycan to tell me just what his desires are, what he's capable of, but something tells me he won't.

"I don't think you're ready for that conversation, little red," he chuckles before he continues eating, and I realize the talk is over. I focus on my plate and attempt to enjoy the meal, which is delicious, but the churning in my gut has my thighs squeezing together with memories.

I recall my ex-boyfriend, a good guy for all intents and purposes, but he was also someone who never could understand how my mind worked when it came to sex. I wanted him to grip me harshly, to spank me, to make me cry out, but his sweet nature had made him soft. Nothing wrong with that, I cared about him, but he wasn't a man who could get me off. After our dates, I would race to my bedroom to grab a vibrator to find pleasure with the dark fantasies that ran through my mind.

And now, I may have found my match, only, he *bought* me from my father. That's not how I wanted to meet the man I'm going to marry. I promised him the week, which I can do. There's no reason I shouldn't give him a chance to prove his worth.

But I just don't know if I'll survive a lifetime.

LYCAN

When breakfast ended, Scarlett disappeared upstairs. I wanted to confess everything to her. Tell her about my proclivities, and even though I'm certain she'll be able to handle them, I didn't. The more I open up to her, the more likely she is to use something against me.

I can't trust her.

I shouldn't trust her.

My office door swings open, and Kahn saunters in dressed all in black. His heavy boots thud against the wooden floorboards as he nears my desk. I watch him silently as he slips into the high, wingback chair that faces me.

"Darius is in New York. He's been meeting with the Capo of the Moretti *familia*. There's something

114

odd going on. Why would he be talking to Alex's cousins?"

That's a good fucking question. I don't respond to Kahn; instead, I pick up my mobile and hit dial on Alexei's number. I'll get the truth, one way or another.

"What can I do for you, Shaw?" Alex's thick accent comes across the speaker after one ring.

Leaning back in my chair, I tell him, "My brother and your cousin seem to be buddies. Any reason why?" I'm not afraid of Alex. I've known him far too long to fear him, but I wouldn't want to get on the wrong side of him.

"Interesting. I'm not sure." Papers shuffle on the other side of the line before he speaks again. "Looks like Franco has him running a job down to Miami. I can get the details on it if you'd like."

"I would. Darius is volatile. I don't trust him. He may be blood, but he hasn't been family for a long time." With the job Kahn's doing for Alex, looking into the church and convent, I don't want anything to come between my relationship with the mafia, but I can't have them working with the one man I *don't* trust.

"I understand. Give me an hour. I'll speak with the cousins and see what is happening on their end. I haven't been in the Big Apple for long enough to have met with them yet. Perhaps it's time I pay my *familia* a visit." Amusement laces his tone, but I'm too fucking wired to join him.

"Thank you. I'm with Kahn now. I'll have an update on the convent in your email soon."

"A pleasure as always," Alex says before hanging up. My gaze is locked on my right-hand man, needing some form of distraction from my thoughts of breakfast with Scarlett.

"I want to go in, undercover." Kahn's deadly serious expression is the only clue that he's ready to kill. Everything else about him seems calm, laid back. If I didn't know him, I would've said he's sitting with a friend, chatting about drinks tonight or the woman he fucked this morning.

"Give me a couple of days." I pick up the folder and slide it over to the edge of the desk nearest to him. "The contract is signed. All I need is our little princess to agree, put her signature on the dotted line, and I'll happily have you go do anything you need to. But she's still a flight risk."

"You think she'll run?"

"I do. All the way back to grandmother's house." The link to an old fairytale isn't lost on me. This, however, isn't fiction. This is real life, and Scarlett Bardot now belongs to the big bad wolf.

"I'll stay in the cottage until you're ready. The team is waiting on my order," Kahn informs me as he flicks through the information I got for him.

"It seems Lorenzo has taken up residence in the convent. He's playing the good priest while he uses the women who come to him for help as toys in a much bigger game."

My blood runs hot through my veins. I can't imagine what Kahn is going through. His sister was taken when she was sixteen, stolen as she was walking home from school, and we haven't had a link to finding her for years. But it seems we've made a breakthrough.

"I want to be there when you take him down," I tell him. I'm not someone who has friends, have never been, but if I did call someone a friend, it would be Kahn. "I want to watch as he pays the price for his indiscretions."

A small, yet sadistic smile curls Kahn's lips. Fire blazes in his dark eyes as he regards me, excitement painting his expression like the goddamned Joker. He may not have bright green hair or clown makeup on, but there's something dark in the way his gaze brightens with dangerous intent.

"Of course," he agrees with a quick nod. "I wouldn't have it any other way. Unless you're on your honeymoon by then, enjoying the spoils of a long-awaited victory," he tells me, leaning his elbows on his knees. "I have to be honest; if you didn't claim her, I wouldn't mind taking her just to see the look on her father's face."

"I think perhaps I should have her visit Heaven," I ponder out loud. "Maybe she'll get a glimpse of what her father is really like. She'll finally know the truth about just how far he'll go to get his kicks." *And how far I'll go to have her bound in my playroom.*

"I think that sounds like a brilliant idea." Kahn pushes to his feet. "I better get going. Have a few things to do before I meet up with some of the guys tonight. I can't persuade you to join us. Can I?"

I shake my head. As much as I would like to let loose, have a few bourbons before coming home to Scarlett, I think it's time I showed her what she would be giving up if she walked away. "No. I need to spend time with her, to get her to trust me before the gala."

"Are you sure taking her there is a good idea?" Kahn's brows furrow with worry, and I want to say no, I don't think it's a good idea, but I can't keep her away from her grandmother, not forever. Because she needs to learn the truth, and I want it to come from the one person who is guilty of the domino effect that's plagued both families for years.

"I'll ensure she behaves."

He nods before leaving me to think about my plans for tonight. I pick up my mobile and hit dial on another number, one I haven't called in a very long time. I wait for the rings, counting them when they sound.

Once.

Two.

Three.

"Mr. Shaw," comes the voice that sends anger scouring through every vein in my body.

"Grace Bardot," I utter her name, hoping the contempt is clear to her. "Your granddaughter is quite the spitfire," I tell her. She knows where Scarlett is. She knew the moment I brought her into the house. Horatio would have told Grace about the contract because his *mommy* always fixes his fuck ups, but this time, she has no way of remedying her son's mistake.

"She will never marry you. Not because I forbid it, but my granddaughter is not stupid to fall for the likes of you." Venom laces every word she spews. She's trying to come across as formidable, but she's nothing more than a wounded animal trying to throw me off the scent.

"Like you did with my father?" I challenge easily, earning me a gasp in response. I knew she'd tell me I'm bad news, even though she knows I've never denied it. The woman is a viper, one that can easily strike, but she has nothing on me. Whereas I know what kind of man her son is, and I can take him down without blinking.

"The past is in the past," she warns. "But the

curse still lies in wait. For years we've fought it, and when Conall died, I thought it would die with him."

"A curse is a way for the elders attempting to stop us from ever loving, but you have no reason to fear. I'm not capable of love." And it's true. I may find Scarlett attractive, alluring even, but my heart has been solidified, and nothing will ever change that.

"Don't ever discount the strength of a family curse."

Anger takes over as her words ring in my ears. I've always wanted the truth, wanted her to admit what she did. But she never has. In all our altercations in New York, she's never once allowed me the freedom from pain by revealing the truth. But now that I have her on the phone, just us, I ask, "Is that what you told my father when you had him killed?"

The silence on the other end of the line is deafening. There's no denying it, and there's no admitting it. But one day, and one day soon, I'll find out the truth.

"Make no mistake, Grace, I will marry your granddaughter. She'll take my name, and once that's done, the Bardot line will be nothing more than a distant memory."

"Scarlett will attend the gala, as planned." The hint of pain in her voice is unmistakable. If there's one thing I've learned over the years, it's that someone like Grace Bardot, who comes from old money, is filled with far too much pride to ever allow anything to get to her. To break her down. But she knows I'm a formidable match. And I'll happily step into the ring and fight her to the death.

Not mine.

But hers.

"She will." I nod to myself. "But if you even think of saying anything about our agreement, there will be consequences. And trust me when I say I always get what I want."

"You're just like him, you know," she tells me, her voice lowering to nothing more than a whisper. "Charming. Handsome. And yet, you're still trying to prove yourself."

My chest tightens at her words. The reminder that I lost my father is a steel blade in my chest. I know what was taken from me because I was old enough to know the man who raised me, who taught me everything I know, and then the Bardots took that.

"Don't ever speak of him," I sneer, my free hand tightening into a fist at the thought of finding my father's body, lifeless, blood dripping from fatal wounds. "You have no reason to even think about him. If I could remove him from your mind, I would."

This time, she offers a sigh before speaking. "I'm sure you're capable of it, but you wouldn't hurt the family of the woman you're about to marry."

"Is that a challenge, Grace?" I can't help but chuckle. She knows I won't back down. And she knows I'm capable of far worse than her mind can even ponder.

"She won't forgive you." This is true. There's no doubt in my mind.

"And I'll never forgive you."

SCARLETT

When a knock comes on my bedroom door at six in the evening, I pad to it and pull it open before I have time to rethink it. On the threshold is Lycan in a pair of dark jeans and a light-blue button-up. The cuffs have been rolled up to his elbows while the top three buttons are undone, offering me a glimpse of smooth, tanned skin.

"Hi." Those perfectly formed lips curl into a friendly smile before he continues, "I have dinner ready and was wondering if you'd like to join me."

"Is that an order or an invite?" I test, offering him a glimpse of a grin before I school my features. He could just pick me up and walk down to the dining room with me, but he doesn't.

"It's an invite to join your fiancé for a meal.

We'll sit on the patio. It's a lovely evening with the fire blazing," he informs me. "Meet me in fifteen minutes. Choose something pretty from the closet." He gives me a slight nod before making his way down the hall, leaving me staring at the empty doorway.

Once I shut myself in the bedroom again, I race to the closet to find something to wear. Thankfully, I had time to shower earlier and wash my long, wavy, red hair. The length almost hitting the base of my spine.

Flicking through the hangers, I find simple black pants with a matching long-sleeved, red blouse. It's as if the whole wardrobe has been designed in outfits rather than items. I dress quickly before adding a dab of pink gloss to my lips. I line my eyes with black kohl and run the brush through my unruly hair.

I'm not sure why I'm nervous, but the flurry of wings in my belly is enough to have me giggling like a teenager about to head on her first date. I wish for a moment I could talk to Aelin and tell her what's happened. Perhaps tonight I can ask Lycan if I could get my phone. I'm almost certain she's sent out a search party for me. But then again, she might be partying in the city with enough guys to keep her busy for months.

Once I've breathed deeply to calm my nerves, I leave my bedroom and head downstairs to the hall to the dining room, where we spent breakfast together. The meal was tense but seeing Lycan do something so *normal* was eye-opening.

When I promised to give him a week to allow him to prove he's not a monster, I didn't think it would be possible. Yet each interaction with him has been filled with sexual tension rather than animosity. He's been polite, almost gentlemanly.

But even so, I'm not about to go tripping over myself because he's nice to me. It doesn't change the fact that he only has me here because of my father. And that's also something I need to learn more about. I have to know what's happened between the two men in my life.

Why did my father force Lycan's hand?

Did he know what would happen to me?

By the time I reach the glass doors that have been opened, allowing the cool evening breeze to sweep through the dining room, I have more questions than ever before. But what I find waiting for me takes my breath away.

The pillars that form a picturesque frame to the garden have been strung with white fairy lights. The table set for two has four tealight candles dancing in the gentle breeze. And the two place settings are perfect, waiting for us to take our seats.

Lycan picks up a wine glass from the cotton

tablecloth and hands it to me. The red liquid shimmers under the soft illumination. If I were ever to tell someone about my dream date, this would be it. It's as if Lycan has burrowed himself in my mind and stolen every thought I've had about spending an evening with someone I care about and made it real.

"Welcome," he says as I take the glass from him. With a sip of my drink, I allow the warmth of the fruity, yet spicy alcohol to soothe the bird's wings that have taken flight in my stomach.

"This is beautiful," I remark as I slip into the waiting chair Lycan's pulled out for me. He helps me with the seat before taking his own. Lifting his glass, he holds it up over the dancing flames, and I mimic his action.

"To a new beginning," he says before clinking his glass against mine. The crystal tinkling while his gemstone eyes twinkle with mischief.

"Is this your way of attempting to soften me to the idea of marrying you?" I challenge before taking another mouthful of wine, hoping it will keep me calm through the dinner. Before Lycan can answer, we're joined by his staff, who bring out plates with steaming food, waiting to be devoured. I notice the girl from this morning isn't one of our servers, and I want to ask about her, but I don't.

It's not my place. Not yet anyway. Once we're

alone, I take in the meal in front of me—a bed of lettuce with small, bright red tomatoes, cucumber, and herbs. There are roasted cubes of pumpkin and steamed potatoes surrounding a beautifully prepared piece of chicken. My stomach growls in response, and a chuckle has me lifting my gaze to find Lycan watching me intently.

"I hope you enjoy dinner," he tells me. "I didn't think to ask if you're allergic to anything. Forgive me." He tips his head to the side in apology, and I can't help but take in the shadows that dance across his face from the flames.

"Oh, no, I'm not. I pretty much eat anything." We settle in after that, eating in comfortable silence, and for the first time since I was brought here, I feel *normal*. Perhaps it's a mistake to allow myself the liberty of not being scared or worried about what's going to happen, but knowing we're right next door to Gran's house also sets me at ease.

"Your grandmother is looking forward to the gala," Lycan says as we're halfway through our meals. This causes me to snap my focus on him.

"You spoke to her?" Disbelief laces my tone because she hasn't even bothered to talk to me or even ask after me. Surely, she's concerned about me being here.

"I did. I gave her a call earlier to let her know you're well." I'm staring at Lycan, mouth gaped in shock at his cavalier attitude. "I've known her a long time," he continues in between bites of his dinner. "She's a formidable woman."

"Why did you not allow me to speak to her?"

"You'll see her soon enough," he tells me before popping a forkful into his mouth. His jaw works as he chews, his shrewd gaze locked on me. Suddenly, my appetite has dissipated into a swirl of anger, not at Lycan this time, but at my grandmother.

Instead of finishing my half-eaten meal, I pick up my wine and gulp down what's left before glancing at Lycan, who's holding the bottle ready to fill up my glass. I allow him to before drinking down half of what he poured. Anger sluices through me at how my family can just allow me to be taken.

"I'm sorry," Lycan says suddenly, causing me to focus on him instead of swirling the crimson liquid in my glass. "Sometimes family isn't always what you expect them to be."

"Like with your brother?" I throw out, remembering how he warned me against the man who chased me through the woods. *The hunter who wanted to steal me.* The thought has a cold shiver skittering down my spine.

"Yes." It's only one word, but it's drenched in agony and rage. Lycan doesn't look at me as he finishes his meal before lifting the white napkin to wipe his mouth. Once he's done, he sits back, drink in hand, to stare out at the dark garden beyond our idyllic setting. "There were times when I was younger, after my father died, that I believed Darius would come home."

"I'm sorry you had to lose two people you loved." For a moment, he looks human. Almost. I guess grief makes people seem more real because it's only then they allow you to see inside them. The pain takes hold, and the walls they build come crashing down, even if only for a short moment. And that's what I glimpse in Lycan now. The heartbroken young man, not the wolf who could devour me whole.

"Love is merely an empty promise," he murmurs before sipping his drink. The wine staining his lips blood-red. "It's a word people throw around when there's nothing more to say or when they feel as if they're losing the game of life."

"That's not a way to look at it."

This time, he pins me with those emerald orbs. "Isn't it?" His dark brow arches, his jaw ticking as he regards me, and those beautiful eyes glimmer with a challenge.

"No. Because love makes you strong, it makes you fight for what's right." Even as I say it, I feel like a martyr because I've never been in love. I've only read about it in romance novels, which, to be fair, are all fiction. I don't know the depth of passion in my own right, only what I've come to learn from the heroes within the pages of a book.

"You're one of those girls who wants the knight in shining armor to save you," Lycan remarks. "I'm not that. I never will be." Darkness crosses over his face. His eyes hold danger, and even though I should be scared, I'm not.

"I don't need a knight to save me," I bite out, frustration at being called out, lancing my chest, causing my cheeks to heat, and I pray he can't see my embarrassment stained on my face.

"Next time you're in danger, and you're thinking about what you can do to get out of it, I want you to recall this moment. Remember the words you uttered because I may not be a knight, but if anything happens to you, I'll be there," Lycan informs me. "And only when you finally admit you're mine will I kill everyone in my path to keep you safe." He tips his glass toward me in a cheer before he swallows back the last of his drink. His throat works as he swallows, and I can't help but watch him with anger and desire fueling my blood.

I'm not sure how to respond to his promise. Instead of speaking, I nod and finish my drink. The staff appears again as if on cue, removing the plates and replacing them with small bowls of gelato and a bottle of bubbly, which Lycan proceeds in popping open.

He silently fills two flutes before setting the bottle in the ice bucket brought out with our dessert. Everything has been thought out tonight; he planned this, and even though I'm a whirlwind of emotion, I allow myself to enjoy the moment.

I pick up my spoon and scoop some of the cool ice cream into my mouth. Flavors of candy burst on my tongue—vanilla and strawberries—and a moan of pleasure vibrates in my throat. When my lashes flutter open once more, Lycan is beside me, on his knee, holding out a small, black velvet box. I don't need to open it to know there's a ring inside. And the way those green eyes are locked on me, holding out a hope of want and desire, I realize this isn't just *any* dinner — this is a proposal.

"I didn't think of doing this until this afternoon when I was sitting in my office alone," he tells me. "I wasn't going to because our marriage isn't what you would call traditional."

"No, it's not at all."

"But I would like you to wear this ring," Lycan says, popping the lid on the box. The silky pillow that holds a gold ring topped with a heart-shaped ruby sits waiting for me. It's beautiful, simple, yet elegant in every way. It's perfect.

"It's like you've read my mind," I blurt before thinking it through. My admission makes Lycan smile as he pulls out the ring, holding it out to me.

131

I could refuse him right now, I could tell him to go to hell and try to run, but until I've spoken with my grandmother and my father, I don't know what my future holds.

With a slow nod, I allow Lycan to slip the ring on my finger. It's heavy, weighting my hand down as the sparkling jewel now confirms I'm going to be his. *A week*. That's what I promised.

"If in a week you want to take it off, you're welcome to. I always keep my word," he tells me, once more making me think he can read my mind. If he can, he'll know how at war I am with myself over this situation. Lycan picks up the champagne glasses, offering me one, which I accept. "Here's to a future which neither of us expected." He sips his drink as I do mine, and our gazes never falter. And for a moment, he allows me in to see the man inside. The one who lost a father, who has an estranged brother. A man who's as unsure of his place with me as I am of my place with him.

In this moment, my heart stutters.

He seems human.

But as quickly as it flickers in his eyes, it's gone in the next second. And I wonder if he'll ever allow me in fully.

LYCAN

I wanted nothing more than to spend the night with her. Seeing her wearing my ring, I was overcome with pride that I have her on my side. Perhaps not fully—yet. But soon, she'll come to realize I'm not a man who takes no for an answer. And I will whittle away at her defenses until she submits.

As much as I would like to join her for breakfast, I need to talk to the team. Kahn called late last night, informing me that Darius is back. For some reason, he's returned to Crimson Falls, but we can't find the bastard.

Stalking into my office, which is filled with men all dressed in black, I glance around, taking in each one. They're anxious, just like I am. The air in the room is twisted with the need for violence.

We should've been locked in a meeting all night, but even after Kahn's call, I couldn't bring myself to sit around talking about my brother. But we need to figure out the best way to lure Darius out.

The night I brought Scarlett here, I knew he would linger, and when the two security guards I keep onsite slinked into the night, through the forest and into the Bardot garden, they found the cottage beside the house empty. A note waited for me on the wooden table, one that caused my blood to heat.

He'd disappeared once again.

I can't afford to waste time looking for him while I have a girl upstairs who could either stand by my side or end up running. The wedding needs to go ahead, but I also need her to be on my side when the gala happens in a few days. Even though she's now wearing my ring, there is no guarantee she'll trust me when I haven't given her a reason to.

There's so much more to the story than she can fathom.

But it's not entirely my story to tell.

Kahn's gaze locks on mine the moment I slide into my chair. "He's close, and I have a feeling he'll make an appearance at the gala. I can go hunt him down," Kahn says, his stare on mine, waiting for the response he knows is coming. This is what he was trained to do. It's something he loves. There's no doubt in my mind, if I were to nod, he would be out there in an instant, his predatorial instincts kicking in, and his team right behind him.

My memory leaps back to Scarlett questioning me in her bedroom about the shot she heard the night he chased her through the forest. When I walked out into the garden that night, gun in hand, I didn't expect Darius to be hanging around, but then I noticed him hidden amongst the trees, waiting. I took a chance. I pulled the fucking trigger but missed.

He isn't back at the Bardot mansion. We now know that. What still doesn't sit right with me is how Grace hired him in the first place. She must know he's a Shaw. There is no denying he is my father's son, and she had to realize who he was when he got the job on her property.

Which begs the question—*what the fuck is Grace Bardot hiding?*

Kahn's watching me, waiting for a response to his comment. If my brother were to die today, I'm not sure I'll feel the pain. Actually, I don't feel anything, not anymore. *Except desire for the girl upstairs.*

My life has been a series of unemotional ties—one-night stands, contractual obligations— all offering nothing more than satisfaction for a moment. I never allowed myself to grow close to someone, to open what's left of my heart, and to have someone burrow themselves into my soul.

Scarlett is merely a means to an end.

She's part of the plan for revenge I will finally claim over her family. There wasn't another way to do this, to make them pay. I push my chair away from the desk and stand. Buttoning my suit jacket, I round my desk after picking up the folder.

"I want to question my brother. A niggling in my gut tells me there's more to this story than I know. He's working with the mafia, but he's also in Grace Bardot's pocket." I glance at each man in the room, all focused on me as I speak. "He's hiding something, or she is. One way or another, I will find out what it is. "I want you to search every fucking corner of this town. Find him, but bring him back alive." The order is clear, and Kahn offers a nod.

The sound of chairs scraping along the wooden floorboards fills the room as each man rises and takes his leave. I don't think it will take long for them to do a sweep of Crimson Falls, and it won't take them long to find him, wherever he's hiding.

Once I'm alone, I head to the patio doors that overlook the garden. The spot where I breached the trees with Scarlett in my arms is right in front of me, and I wonder if she'll ever come to terms with being my wife. Wearing my ring, she may have given me an inch into her thoughts, but there's so much more to break through.

In a few weeks, she'll take my name, and there's nothing she can do about it. I may have given her an out after the week is up, and I'll allow her to think she has a choice, but in actual effect, she's in this to the end.

If she refuses, her father will go to jail, and something tells me it's not what she'd want. Her life has been a series of events planned by her parents who wanted to rule her future. I'm not them. I may have failed to mention she's also here to give me an heir, but if she truly wants her own company, I'll give that to her. Call it repayment because this is a business transaction.

Nothing she's done in her life has been of her own will, and now I'll take the last remaining choice away from her by making her a Shaw.

I should feel bad.

But I don't.

I turn and stalk out into the hallway. The sound of the front door opening alerts me to visitors. Gray steps aside for me to see the tall brunette who's entering my home. The wedding dress designer, Opal, or something like that. Behind her are two younger girls pushing a brass railing with black clothing bags lined up for Scarlett to choose from.

When I selected the options from the website, I had her in mind. As I flicked through the choices, I couldn't help but picture her wearing each one, and that had my dick hard. But what had me stroking myself was the thought of ripping the material from her body on our wedding night and claiming her.

"Mr. Shaw, I'm Opal," the designer greets with a smile and an offered hand as I near them. "I trust you're well." Her dark eyes are filled with excitement, only because I told her money is no limit.

"I am. Thank you for making the trip on such short notice. My bride is rather stressed about the wedding, and I'd like to take as much off her plate as possible." I gesture for her to follow me down to the dining room. With the curtains open, the sunshine streams through, offering a bright space to revel in the elegant gowns. I've ensured the staff have moved furniture around for this very reason. The room is large enough for Scarlett to try on the dresses, and the full-length mirror I had brought in from one of the guest rooms is ready and waiting.

"Thank you," Opal says. "I'll get ready if you'd like to bring her down."

Nodding, I make my way up to my fiancée's bedroom, knowing that this will end up in a fight. Scarlett hasn't warmed to the idea of marrying me yet, and even though I understand why she needs to submit, or I will be forced to *make* her bend to my will.

I push open the door to find her at the window seat. Her head snaps toward me, her eyes wide. I take in her outfit, the knee-length white socks hiding her beautiful calves, along with a pair of light blue sleep shorts which tease at a glimpse of her panties underneath.

Her top is floppy, hiding her tits from view, but I know what's under the material. I've glimpsed her bikini photos on social media. When I was doing my research, I made sure to study each and every picture, so I'll know my bride inside and out.

I raise a hand toward her. "Come."

Her brows furrow in confusion before she asks, "Where?"

Running my fingers through my hair, I lift my gaze to hers and regard her for a long while. "You're trying on wedding dresses."

"No."

"Scarlett, if you continue acting like this, I can just bind you to the wall and have them dress you while I watch." The thought of her bound to a St. Andrew's cross flits through my mind, and I have to stifle the groan of pleasure that rumbles in my chest.

"You're insufferable." Her huff is nothing more than a taunting grumble, but the sound of frustration that escapes her lips makes me want nothing more than to bend her over and spank the insolence from her.

"And you're mine. Now come, I don't have all day to stand here arguing with you."

Scarlett rolls her chocolate-brown eyes in annoyance as she pushes off the window seat and pads barefoot toward me. She's tiny without shoes on, and I can't help but want to pick her up, haul her over my shoulder, and lock her in my bedroom. But that has to wait for our wedding night.

She follows me down the hallway to the staircase, and we silently make our way into the dining room, where the dresses are now hanging freely. All I see is white lace and satin, along with jeweled tiaras I know will look exquisite on Scarlett.

Only the best for my future wife.

"This is…" Her voice is tinged with awe, her pouty lips parted with shock as she takes in the set up. Her lashes flutter, and those dark-rimmed irises are wide as she looks at every inch of the space before turning her wide gaze to me.

The designer rushes forward with a bright smile on her face. "Welcome, Miss Bardot. I'm Opal. Such a pleasure to meet you. I trust we'll have something to your liking." When Opal glances at me, I nod, taking my leave as I pull the doors shut. But before I disappear, I lock my gaze on Scarlett's and give her a warning glare. *Behave.*

Back in my office, I'm nervous. I've never felt like this before. Usually, I'm calm, relaxed, even when taking down my opposition. But Scarlett does something to me.

She makes me want.

She makes me crave.

She makes me *human*.

And that can never be a good thing.

SCARLETT

The first dress didn't have much material to it, and I have a feeling that Lycan had something to do with that. The second one was pretty, but it wasn't something I would be caught dead in with the almost nonexistent front and back. My cleavage was prominent, far too exposed if he intends to make me walk into a church.

I grew up in the church, going to catechism, learning passages from the Bible until they were ingrained into my mind, never leaving, and even though I don't go every Sunday, there is no way I'll be standing in front of a priest wearing that.

If that's what Lycan wants, he can find someone else to marry.

"Let's try this one," Opal says after I've

undressed for the third time today. She's pretty, and for a split second, I wonder if Lycan's dated her, or if he's been intimate with her. A spike of jealousy crashes through me before I pull myself together and offer her a smile.

"So, how long have you known Mr. Shaw?" I query as I take the slip she's holding out to me. Her gaze lands on mine, but there's no guilt or jealousy in her pretty eyes.

"A few months. He was at one of my fashion shows," she remembers with a smile. "He even offered to donate toward my charity. I have to say, you're very lucky."

My mouth opens, but no words come out. I'm not sure if I am lucky or if my luck had run out, and I was left with a man who *bought* me. "What charity is it?" I ask instead of talking more about my future husband.

Her gaze drops to the floor, and I can tell she's nervous from the way her hands twist in front of her. "I...Uhm... I've always wanted to support women, to show them they're strong, not because they're a wife or mother, but because they're warriors. So, I started up a charity to help women coming from abused homes." This time when she looks up at me, my heart stutters.

"That's amazing." It's the truth. I've heard about women living in fear daily. Women who aren't strong enough to fight back but also feel stuck. "You know," I start, turning to face her fully. "I'd love to interview you. I'm a media relations student, and I'll be interning in New York next month. It would be an incredible story to take to the company."

Opal's eyes widen. Her smile is bright, lighting up her face with excitement. "That is something I would definitely love to do." She grins, and we move back to the mirror, where I look at what I'm wearing.

The material of the sleek, floor-length, satin dress hugs my curves. For some reason, looking at myself in the mirror makes this all too real. As the girls flurry around me like excited hummingbirds, ready to flit into the clear, blue sky, I turn my gaze away from my reflection and out to the garden. I don't want to admit that this feels like some strange and twisted fairy tale.

Every girl dreams of her wedding day. I, for one, never thought I'd marry someone of my own choice. And it's as if those thoughts brought Lycan to me. Because I didn't choose him, and yet here I am, donning a princess dress which looks like it's straight from the pages of a book.

My prince isn't a knight in shining armor but a commanding wolf in an expensive, tailored suit. Once everyone steps back, I realize I was lost in thought, and when I glance at Opal, she's grinning as if she's just won the lottery.

"This is it," she coos as she claps her hands together excitedly. I want to turn, but in the same vein, I want to run and hide. I want them to remove the mirror, so I don't look at just how perfectly this dress fits.

"Are you sure?" I ask, still nervous, keeping my eyes from landing on the glass to my left. She grins wider, nodding quickly as she takes the veil and gestures toward me. I offer her a small smile and tip my head so she can place the bejeweled crown with sheer lace over my hair. It hangs low behind me; the weight of it is astounding.

"Yes. A picture of perfection." She offers me a chef's kiss before stepping back and allowing me space. As much as I don't want to be excited to see the result, I do turn and face the mirror finally. My breath is stolen for a long moment as I look at the woman staring back at me.

Atop the satin shift is a gown made purely of lace. Now I see why I had to put the silky material on first. If I didn't, this would be see-through. The lace covers my chest to my neck. It cinches at my waist before exploding into a wide circle all the way to the shiny marble tiles.

I twist and turn, taking in every angle. The back is completely bare, with thin lace twisting from my shoulders down to the base of my spine, creating a delicate V-shape. The veil hanging down my back looks like it's been made from the most fragile snowflakes with a delicate pattern of unique shapes.

The crown on my head sparkles in the light coming in from the floor-to-ceiling doors to my right. Doors that could lead to my freedom if I ran right now. But I wouldn't get far because I know my captor will not let me go.

Opal picks up a box that was sitting on a chair behind her and brings it to me. "This is for you. I think it will suit the dress." She hands me the gift, a rectangular, merlot-colored box with a red ribbon. When I tug at the bow, it falls away easily, and I lift the lid to find a gold bracelet. When I lift it from the suede cushion, a small charm dangles, and I have to set the box down to get a better look.

"This is gorgeous," I tell her, but my eyes are focused on the charm between my thumb and forefinger. A small, intricately designed wolf with a deep-set green eye, watching me. "This is…"

"Mr. Shaw said that I should give this to you, to wear on the wedding day," Opal tells me. "He left it here with a note." She points to the chair before looking at my shocked face. "Are you okay?"

"Yes, yes, sorry. I think I'm just overwhelmed." I take a step back and slowly move toward the mirror, where I finally allow myself to look, to really look at the woman there. The one staring back at me with

146

her cheeks flushed, her lips pouty, and her eyes sparkling with emotion.

The dress is perfect.

"This is it," I tell myself, but Opal claps excitedly behind me. As much as I want to tell her to save me, to call my father and tell him what's happened, I don't. Instead, I smile. If Lycan wants arm candy, I can be that. If he wants someone who'll run his businesses with him, I can even do that. But if he thinks for one moment he's going to get me to change my name at the end of the month, he's wrong, and I'll show him that.

He may not have *wanted* me before we met, and he may only want this wedding to happen because of some archaic contract, but I'll make him fall in love with me, and then I'll run. I'll escape into the darkness of the forest, and he won't ever find me.

Four weeks until my birthday. It's a long time to let someone in, to feel something for someone, and the moment I see the humanity in his gaze, I'll be the one to strike. I'll end him and this godforsaken agreement my father has allowed.

I'm not a toy.

I'm not a possession.

But I can play the part just as well as anyone.

SCARLETT

By the time I've had a shower, and I'm sitting on my window seat, I'm exhausted. The dress I chose is perfect. It's absolutely breathtaking, and I'm sure Lycan will agree. I catch myself sighing as I wonder why I'm even going ahead with this, even wondering what he'll think. It's not like me to give in, to submit to a man, especially after what he's done to keep me here. But if I'm going to play into his game, get him to love me, and then end this farce, I need to make sure he trusts me, which is why I accepted his ring.

My bedroom door opens with a silent murmur against the plush carpets, and I'm met with one of the maids. Dressed in black and white, she looks to be about my age, or perhaps a few years older. She offers a small smile as she sets down a silver tray with a glass of red wine, along with a white envelope. My name is scrawled in elegant handwriting on the front.

"What's this?"

"Mr. Shaw has requested you have some wine, and also, he's left you a note." Of course, he did. The young woman nods before she leaves me in the room, pulling the door closed behind her. I want to run after the girl and ask her more questions. But I focus on the note instead.

I pick up the envelope, slowly unfolding the flap to pull out the note my fiancé wrote. The immaculate script is beautiful, and I allow my gaze to rove over the perfectly formed letters.

Tonight, you'll dine with me, and perhaps we can take this a step further.

L.

Direct and no-nonsense.

Just like the man himself.

I realize he's someone who doesn't like the word no, and he's also someone who always gets what he wants. If I were to tell him I'm not hungry, or I'd rather eat alone, he'd march up here and lift me over his shoulder, kicking and screaming. And he'd enjoy it too. I'll then be carried down to the dining room. So instead of fighting, I'll follow his rules.

Padding over the carpet, I make my way to the closet to find something to wear. I have an inkling that this isn't going to be a "burger and fries" type of dinner after last night, so I need to ensure I'm elegant, yet sexy. If I want the man to fall in love with me, I should appear to be ready to take the next step with him.

Which brings a thought to my mind—if he wants me as his wife, he'll want sex. Heat coils through me, settling low in my gut as I recall his fingers, how they taunted and teased, how I fell apart as he touched me. His perfectly timed strokes sent me reeling, and I don't doubt he would and could do it again and again.

Flicking through the hangers, I find an emerald satin cocktail dress the same color as Lycan's eyes. The garment is far too exquisite to wear in the house, but I can't help the need coursing through me to impress him, to show him I'm not some stupid girl he can boss around.

I'm a woman.

I take the item into the bedroom and lay it on the bed. Next, I choose lingerie which has been packed in a glass cabinet in the walk-in closet. There's everything from white cotton panties to black and red lace. Picking out a charcoal set, I smile for a moment, wondering if he'll even see this tonight. The bra and panty are made of sheer lace, with thin straps that feel like heaven across my skin.

I find a pair of silver heels I slip on after I've donned the dress. At the vanity, which steals my breath each time I take in the scene of the wolf chasing Red, I settle on the stool and start applying some lip gloss over a nude shade I found in one of the drawers. As I line my eyes with black, I allow my mind to develop a plan of action.

The mascara makes my lashes seem even longer and curled. And when I'm done, I sit back for a moment to summon the courage to face him again. I haven't seen Lycan since he left me in the dining room with Opal. Nervously, I get to my feet and head for the door, which I find still unlocked. In the hallway, it's deathly silent, and I'm thankful for the peace before I have to make conversation with the man who wants to marry me.

I move toward the staircase with ease, taking in the tapestries hanging high against the walls. The home is enormous, just like my grandmother's. I have to ask Lycan if I can talk to her, to see her. With the Bardot Gala coming up quickly, I'm sure she's worried about where I've disappeared to unless Lycan has fed her some story about how I'm spending time with him.

The thought coils in my stomach, anger flaring as I reach the steps and take them slowly, wanting to prolong my alone time. But I can't put this off forever, so when I reach the double doors of the dining room, I stop, inhale a deep, cleansing breath, and release it before I push my way into the vast space.

Everything has been returned to normal. The furniture—table, and chairs—fill the center of the room, allowing the cabinets against the walls to frame the place settings where I spot Lycan at the head of the table.

He's dressed impeccably, just like I knew he would be. His suit jacket is unbuttoned, allowing me a view of his button-up, which is a dark gray, reminding me of storm clouds on a cool winter's day. The color pops against the pitch black of his pants and jacket. I don't miss the fact that he's not wearing a tie, and the top few buttons of his shirt are undone. A glimpse of tanned skin has my mind wandering alone into territory I'd rather steer clear from.

"My soon-to-be wife," he voices, his tone filled with arrogant confidence. His lips quirk as his eyes hungrily rove over me. He takes in my long, red waves, then his heated stare burns its way over my face, to my lips, and down, finding my cleavage just peeking out from the neckline of the dress.

When he reaches my legs, he lifts his fist to his mouth and stifles a cough before coming toward me. His long strides swallow up the distance instantly, and seconds later, he's looming over me like a starving predator ready to devour its prey.

"You look rather breathtaking this evening," Lycan murmurs in a low, seductive baritone, which has my spine tingling with awareness of just how close he is. His eyes, those gemstones, shine with a ferocious need that heats me from head to toe.

"Thank you," is all I manage before he steps back and offers me his hand. I accept with trembling fingers, and he leads me to a chair to the left of him. He pulls it out, allowing me to settle before pushing it in. Everything is shimmering under the dim yellow bulbs from the chandelier, and even Lycan looks like a dark angel sent from the depths of hell to dine with me tonight.

"How was the dress fitting?" he asks as he waves his hand toward the staff who bring out plates they set down in front of us. The presentation is gorgeous with finely chopped herbs around the edge of the porcelain, and in the center is a miniature bruschetta with smoked salmon and cream cheese. Adorning this beautiful appetizer is a dollop of caviar. I've only ever tried it once but am looking forward to tasting it again.

"It was good," I tell him, meeting those eyes that seem to pierce right through me, searching for something deep within. Something I'm not willing to give him, not yet. But the moment I think it, I realize

I need to offer him more, because if my plan is going to work, Lycan needs to believe this is becoming real. "I found a dress. It's perfect."

"I'm sure it is. Opal informed me she gave you the gift?" I watch him lift his wine glass, press it to his full, pink mouth, and take a long, languid sip. I can't deny he's handsome, more than I could ever have imagined a man to be, but he's the bad guy.

"Yes. Thank you." I turn my focus onto my food and lift the starter to my mouth to take a bite. As my teeth sink in, the flavors burst on my tongue. An involuntary moan vibrates in my throat, and when my gaze finds Lycan's, heat burns in those gemstones.

"I've always enjoyed watching a woman feast. There's something so erotic about it," he murmurs. A small quirk at the corner of his mouth makes him look like a starving beast rather than a man.

"Oh?" I ask after swallowing the last bite. "Is that a line you use on all your women?" I taunt, causing fire to blaze in his stare. My stomach coils with both anxiety at taunting the wolf and desire at wanting him. Confusion twists its way through me like a coiling serpent about to strike. I can't allow myself to fall into his trap.

"*All* my women don't dine with me," Lycan offers. "Yes, there are some who have accompanied me to parties, but none have seen the inside of my personal space. My home is mine."

"So, you've never brought a woman home?" Incredulity thrums through the words, vibrating each syllable with confusion. He's a handsome, wealthy bachelor, one who must have women falling over themselves to be with him.

"I'm not into relationships. I prefer…" He lifts his fingers to his lips, tapping on them gently as he considers what to tell me. And I find myself leaning forward, intrigued by how he's about to explain his confession. "Women who aren't around for very long."

"So, you prefer escorts who leave after the deed is done?" Once again, I sound like I'm judging him, and perhaps I am in some way. I don't have any right to, but the anxiety that took hold of me earlier turns to an emotion I cannot admit I'm feeling.

A chuckle falls free from Lycan's mouth, his lips parted in a way that allows me a glimpse of pearly whites, while his face lights up in amusement. "No, little red," he says. "I don't pay women to fuck me." His voice turns to lava, burning through every inch of my body, causing goosebumps to flare over my skin. "They beg, they plead, and they find bliss while I taunt and tease." His gaze, locks on mine, and I'm caught in his web. I can't turn away. "Would you like that, little red?"

My mouth pops open, but I can't find the words.

I'm saved when the staff returns, clearing our plates and bringing in the main course. I'm pleasantly surprised to find a bed of couscous covered with stir-fried vegetables. To the side is a thick, juicy steak, along with a salad made of lettuce, tomato, more herbs, and olives.

Once we're alone, I feel his eyes on me, watching my reaction to dinner. Instead of looking at him, I focus on the plate and say, "This looks delicious."

"It certainly does." His response is low, gravelly, but I don't have to lift my head to know he's watching me. And his words have nothing to do with the meal before us. Lycan leans back in his chair but doesn't deter his gaze from me. It's as if flames of desire lick at my skin, traveling from my hand, teasing their way up to my wrist, forearm, and bicep. By the time they reach my shoulder, I shiver at the heat.

I'm not sure I can play this game with him. He's far more experienced. There's no way in hell I could ever win if he does this to me if I allow him to affect me in such a way. My lashes flutter when I feel his nearness reach for me. His hand lands on mine in a commanding gesture, and I realize why. I'd been trembling, holding the fork as it tinkled against the fine porcelain.

"You were rather calm walking in here, little red," he says, his voice taking on the tone of a commanding officer speaking to a soldier readying himself for the front line. "And for a moment, I thought you were finally coming to terms with the wedding. I thought" — he pauses for a moment before continuing — "that you were willing to be my wife, allowing me to finally claim you."

His words incite anger through me. A spark igniting the kindling in my gut, causing me to tug away from him, shoving my chair back against the cool, marble tiles. The clatter of cutlery on the table bounces against the walls, echoing in a poignant warning.

"You're the rogue in this story, Lycan Shaw," I point out. "Being kidnapped by a man doesn't make me want to fall in love with him. It doesn't even make me want to try." My plan is in the gutter. I should've ignored his jeer, but my stubbornness wouldn't allow it.

"I never said anything about love," he comments, folding his arms across his chest, making his shoulders seem even larger with bunched-up muscles. Strength and dominance are what this man wears, like a goddamned cologne. "Sit."

"No."

Lycan's hand's fist on the table. His jaw ticks with frustration as his usually jade irises turn almost black as he regards me. "Scarlett, you must mistake me for a man who doesn't mind the word *no*," he speaks slowly, clearly, and every word is drenched in barely constrained anger. "When I give you an order, you will obey me without question, without sass, and most certainly without that stubborn demeanor you insist on portraying."

He doesn't rise. He sits, still, very fucking still. He reminds me of a predator, lying in wait for the prey to run, because a man like Lycan Shaw enjoys the chase. I can see it glimmer in his stare. The way he's taking in my posture, my stance, he can tell I'm about to bolt out of this room.

"Run." Lycan jerks his chin toward the door just as his lashes flutter with excitement dancing in those dark depths. "I like the chase." His tone drops to almost a whisper, one that's heavy with desire and laced with a threat. One that tells me he will catch me, and I may not like what he does then.

Without another thought, my feet move, and I'm racing toward the patio door, which is ajar, instead of the door leading into the rest of the house. The night breeze hits me as I step out onto the cobbled patio, and my heels click onto the stone, but I focus on the garden. My mind flits through my options, and I quickly make my way deeper into the darkness and away from the house.

"I know this property very well, little red," Lycan warns in amusement and condescension. For a moment, I hate him with a fiery passion, and I want nothing more than to turn around and slam my fist into his face. But I know that won't do anything but hurt me.

My legs carry me out onto the lawn, and I'm thankful my heels aren't sinking into the ground. It's firm, allowing me to run faster than I anticipated. Instinct has me wanting to turn around, but I don't. Instead, I wonder how I can get off his property. Going into the woods isn't an option, so perhaps I can find somewhere to hide.

Heavy footfalls follow me. Even though I'm not faster than he is, he doesn't come near me yet. My heart catapults into my throat when I hear a howl from deep in the woods. There's nothing but darkness ahead, so I turn to my left and race toward the pool house. If I can get around it, perhaps I can hide somewhere. Maybe there's a shed hidden in the shadows.

But by the time I slink behind the large structure, my lungs are struggling to pull in air. My hands are shaking as I feel my way around the wall, smooth concrete against my palm. With every minuscule step I take, tension radiates through me. Leaning against the wall, I close my eyes and attempt to focus my hearing on the man following me.

Even though I don't hear him running or even walking, it doesn't mean he's not near me. I'm almost certain he's close, and that means I have to find somewhere to disappear. Straight ahead leads to more of the backyard, with what looks like wooden poles sticking up from the ground. I should've explored outside earlier, but stupidly, I thought I could do this.

I thought I was strong.

My heart cracks at the thought of me losing my life because of my immature thoughts. A scraping sound startles me, and I almost scream into the night, but my hand shoots out to cover my mouth, and I shut my eyes so tight, hoping that it was all just my imagination. Even though I know it wasn't.

Quickly, I slip off my heels and take a tentative step toward the grass that leads out to where I'm guessing the kitchen door would be. I move silently onto the softer, mushier lawn, finding my feet in soggy soil. Either they've just watered here, or I'm about to sink into quicksand. The thought makes me giggle inwardly as I note how far I have to go before I reach what looks like a shed in the distance.

Another step.

And another.

But the moment I reach the first wooden pole, I'm slammed into the soft, wet ground by a heavy, warm body. A scream pierces the night, and Lycan's warm breath is at my ear.

LYCAN

Her body wriggles underneath me. My hand covering her mouth is warm from her short, nervous breaths, and her legs kick upward, but she's pinned beneath me, and she's not going anywhere. I can't help but smile when her ass wiggles against my crotch, causing my cock to harden with need. From the moment I first saw her in her parents' dining room, I knew she was going to fight this. I could tell. But now that I have her, I'm enjoying the taunt and tease we're doing.

"Are you going to behave?" I ask, even as she kicks at me. Her hands attempt to push herself up, but the ground is soft, muddy, and I'm sure the dress she's wearing is completely ruined. Not that I care because all I can think about right now is ripping it from her body and finally claiming her. I release my hold over her mouth, only to be met with a slew of curse words that have me chuckling.

Gripping her wrists, I pull them down to her sides, holding her steady as I push myself up on the slippery ground. Her face is dirty, her hair caked with mud, but she's never looked more beautiful to me.

"Let me go, you fucking monster!" Her voice is wrenched from her throat, so loud it echoes into the darkness. Thank fuck I let the gardener leave for the week to see his family. When the door to the small structure where he stays opens and Kahn steps out into the night, I can't help but laugh at his expression of shock.

"What do we have here?"

"Help me, please," Scarlett pleads as she looks up at him, walking toward us. I still have her pinned down, and filthy thoughts of having her bound to my bed infiltrate my mind.

"Oh, sweetheart," Kahn says. "My boss isn't a man I'd like to cross. As pretty as you are, I think it's best you obey him and not tempt him by playing a game of cat and mouse." Kahn drops to his haunches to take in the girl beneath me. A flicker of interest sparks in his gaze, but it's gone in the next second, and I'm thankful because I don't feel like killing my right-hand man.

Scarlett wriggles some more, attempting to tug her arms from my hold, but she's too small, too delicate to fight her way free. I lean in, my gaze on Kahn's when I whisper in her ear. "Would you like to play with us, little red?" I don't wait for her response before continuing. "I'm not usually one to share, but if you're feeling particularly *filthy*, I'm happy to oblige just this once."

"Fuck you!" Her words are spat with venom and malice, which get lost in the darkness because even though I should be hurt, I'm not. Emotions don't come into play with her, and I'm almost certain she knows it too.

That's what I tell myself. And that's the story I'll continue telling myself.

"If that's what you're offering, I'll bite," I inform her, keeping my gaze on Kahn. "Your bite first?" I ask him, nudging my cock against the crease of her ass. I know she can feel the hardness against her, and a small whimper of something between pleasure and pain tumbles from her plump lips.

"I think she wants to get dirty with us, boss," Kahn remarks while reaching for her hair, his fingers fisting into the matted strands, and I can't help but chuckle quietly. She feels it. She feels me. The vibration of my body rumbling through hers.

"Let me go, you monster," Scarlett announces, but she doesn't move. Instead, her body stills, almost

163

as if she's giving up, but I'm not going to get played like a sap. She's waiting for me to lighten my hold on her, and then she'll strike. I'm not sure with what energy she'll do this, but knowing my little red, she'll find it within herself to pounce. And fuck, if that doesn't make me what to claim her even more.

When I finally let up, lifting my body from hers, I tug her from the filthy ground and pull her into my hold. Her gaze is locked on Kahn, probably waiting for him to say or do something, but all he offers is a mock salute before he gestures with a tip of his head toward us, leaving us in the darkness.

"Did you think you were having fun running from me, little red?" I question in her ear, my arms wrapped around her like a vise. She can't escape because she's mine.

"Don't think for one second you'll ever get me to submit to your games," Scarlett hisses, but she doesn't struggle against me like she was earlier. Instead, she's placated, her body lax, and for a moment, I enjoy her warmth.

Perhaps, with time, she'll come to love me. Even though I'm not capable of that kind of emotion with someone, I'll make sure she's safe, taken care of, and she will never want for anything when she's with me. I don't tell her this; instead, I slip my hand in hers, tangling our fingers together, and tug her along behind me.

I focus on the rage coursing through me instead of desire. Both emotions warring in my chest, in my mind. On the one hand, all I want to do is punish her with my hand, with my belt, and then my cock. On the other, I want to bind her to the bed until she finally submits. Until she realizes there is nowhere to run.

"Wait, please," Scarlett says as I step up onto the porch, where she stumbles behind me. I halt all movement, twisting around so I can face her. With the soft yellow glow of the lamps that illuminates the area, I'm awed at her beauty. I've known she was beautiful since the moment I laid my eyes on her, but seeing her messed, muddy, and broken like this is a new vision that makes my cock throb behind my zipper.

"Let me make something clear, Ms. Bardot," I bite out, allowing the anger to drench my words. "If you attempt that once more, I won't think twice about allowing Kahn to show you what he's capable of. He's been my right-hand man for many years now, and he knows my tastes vary, even though sharing may not be top of the list, but I'll gladly watch as he puts you through your paces."

"I'm not some horse you can train," she grits, her teeth clenching, and I realize she's trying not to lose her mind at me. "I just need to know the reasons. I have to."

"What you *have* to do is obey me when I speak. There are things that you don't know about yet, and I will allow you the knowledge when you're ready."

"I am ready now," she insists, her eyes sparking with curious need and ferocious interest. "Please?" This time, the word is a plea that turns my blood hot with need. How I haven't taken her to my bed yet is a mystery. It's only been a few days, but I have to admit, she's more alluring than I expected.

"I'll tell you when you're ready." Turning for the door, I tug her behind me, and I'm sure the trail of mud we're leaving in our wake will be gone by morning. The staircase will be caked with footprints, but all I can think about is locking her in the bedroom until she's had time to consider what she just did.

By the time we reach Scarlett's bedroom, she's practically vibrating beside me when I stop at the doorway and tug her until her back hits the smooth wooden panel. With my free hand, I tip her chin up, so those pretty eyes are on mine.

"I'm not the monster in your story, even though you've clearly made me out to be." I want to tell her about her father, but that would be going against the agreement we came to. Horatio requested that he be the one to tell her the sordid secrets he'd been keeping. And even though I didn't want him to, he's her father, and the fuck up he's made is his confession to spill.

I doubt she'll ever give him the redemption he seeks, but I'm sure he'll beg and plead, just to get back in his daughter's good graces. But I know for a fact, she'll never again see him the way she does now or did before he signed the contract, offering me her hand in marriage.

"Monsters all want us to believe they're nothing more than heroes. But what makes a man a villain in a story is how he conducts his business and how he treats a lady."

"Are you claiming to be a lady, little red?" I allow a smirk to curl my lips as Scarlett's muddy hand attempts to make contact with my face, but I'm faster. I'll always be quicker than her. And that's something my sweet girl needs to remember.

"You know, Lycan Shaw, just when I think you're finally showing your true, gentlemanly colors, you go and say something like that which convinces me that you're nothing more than a monster." She sneers at me, her nose crinkling, and it's the cutest thing I've ever seen. Never once in my life have I thought of a woman being both cute and seductive, but Scarlett portrays both effortlessly.

"I never once claimed to be a gentleman, my sweet," I inform her. It's the truth. My tastes have darkened both my heart and soul and though I may be polite, there's nothing about me that would let a woman think I'm a gentleman. "Tell me something,

Scarlett. If there was anything in this world that could be given to you, anything at all, what would you ask for?"

For a long moment, she considers this, her lashes fluttering against the apples of her cheeks, and even through the smears of mud, I notice her cheeks darken with a soft, pinkish hue. A flicker of something dances in her eyes, but before she answers, it's gone, and suddenly, she's no longer thinking of whatever had crossed her mind.

And her final response is a lie. "Just let me go." Her lips are parted on soft breaths as she shivers when I lean in to inhale her sweet perfume. It reminds me of a rainy morning on an overcast day—fresh, cool, and crisp—but also drenched in dirt. The contradiction is a strangely euphoric fragrance to my senses.

Tipping my head to the side, I grip her chin between my thumb and forefinger and pull her closer, so our lips are barely touching, but close enough for me to inhale as she exhales. Inadvertently connecting us for a moment before I respond, "That's not an option. Try again."

She tries to pull away, but there's nowhere to go. I've pinned her to the door. My body snug against hers. The soft curves allowing my hard ridges to fit perfectly to her body.

"Lycan." She murmurs my name like a

parishioner calling out a prayer to the heavens above. It hits me right in the chest, in a place I didn't think still existed within me. Women I've been with have screamed my name, but never with such pained need. It's as if she's throwing it out there, allowing it to slither under my skin, snaking its way through my veins until it finds the one muscle I've refused to allow to beat since the night my brother left with the woman who scorned me.

SCARLETT

A shiver wracks through me as a lone tear escapes my lashes and trickles its way slowly, gently, down my cheek. Lycan's quick to react, the pad of his thumb tracing the salty emotion before he locks his gaze with mine as fire blazes in his green eyes.

Shock escapes me as a gasp stumbles over my lips at the action. He's so close, watching me, waiting for a reaction, but I'm too tired to say anything more. Fighting now will only anger him, and I'm not sure I can handle punishment under his hand right now.

"I'm tired," I whisper. More so that he'll leave me be, and I'll be able to think about what he said tonight. Not the promise of him and his friend Kahn taking me, making me pay for running, but that there's more at play than I can figure out.

"Tomorrow, little red, I'll come for you. Be ready at nine. Don't be late because I don't appreciate tardiness." His voice, a tone of deep, frustrated gravel forming the words, as if it's been kicked up from tires traveling too fast over the driveway. A reminder that everything about him is dangerous. Confirmation of just how unmatched we are, him being too dark, and me, well, I'm fragile under his hold. Not because I'm a woman, but because just a touch from Lycan as he trails my cheek with his knuckles, and I feel as if I'm about to buckle under the electric current coursing through me.

"Why?" I question in a whisper so soft I'm not sure he heard it. His mouth quirks, a slow, seductive smirk curling his perfect lips as he takes me in, from chin to hairline and down to my mouth where his heated gaze lingers for a long moment. With another movement, he is so close I'm almost certain he's about to claim my mouth with his, and in that few seconds, I want him to. I want to bend to him. I want to leap onto my tiptoes just to feel those full lips on mine.

But he doesn't. And my heart plummets, embarrassment at my thoughts coursing through me. Every inch of my body aches from the stupid escape which the man before me thwarted.

"Tell me, Lycan," I command, attempting to sound stronger, more formidable than just the girl he sees when he looks at me. Because I'm certain that's what I look like right now, dirty and muddy.

He shakes his head slowly, and I'm not sure if it's his answer, or if he's at war with himself trying to figure out what to say to me. He drops his hand from my chin, and I immediately miss the connection. It's stupid and immature to ache for a man who stole me, who had to have a contract just to get me to marry him. And perhaps I'll pay for the insane thoughts I have toward him, but just for now, I allow myself to consider what being his wife would be like.

When Lycan finally steps away, the cool breeze that sweeps away his warmth causes me to shiver. "Get cleaned up." More gravel rumbles in his throat. "Sleep and don't leave your room tonight, or I will be forced to lock you inside." The warning is clear. The mishap of my running from earlier will not happen again, and he'll make sure of it. "Tomorrow, we'll talk." Then he turns and walks away, leaving me staring at his broad back that tapers into a narrow waist. His shirt is filthy with mud, his dark slacks are probably caked in dirt, and his usually shiny shoes are no longer pristine.

When he reaches the far end of the hall, he stops and turns toward me. I expect him to say something, but he doesn't, he only opens the door and walks inside, and I'm left alone in the darkness.

I don't know what he could say to me tomorrow

that would change my feelings about marrying him, but if I'm going to get out of this alive, I'll have to play by the rules. For now, I retreat into my bedroom where I shut the door and make a beeline for the bathroom.

Once the shower is heated and a haze of warmth billows around me, I strip down and step under the spray that has me hissing in pain at the scrapes and cuts from small stones where I had been pinned under Lycan's heavy frame.

The memory steals my thoughts, and an ache low in my gut twists and turns with the promise that the events of him chasing me, pinning me down, could happen again. It probably will. And I find myself squirming at the idea. *Would I want that?* The question hangs in the air, around me, dancing in the steam, and I realize with certainty that I had never felt more alive than when I was under Lycan, begging for him to stop.

Is it something that I would crave once more?
Yes. Yes, it is.

Grabbing the soap and loofah, I lather up to wash away the dirt stuck to my skin. But I know as I clean myself, there's no way I can wash away the touch of the man down the hall—the man who will soon be my husband.

After I wash my hair and rinse the strands, I turn off the taps and step out into the foggy room.

Wiping my hand against the mirror to clear it of condensation, I stare at myself. The woman looking back at me is different somehow. More... confident.

I grab a towel and wrap myself in the fluffiness before heading back into the bedroom and opening the closet to find something to wear. When I was brought to the room for the first time, I didn't think I would find it comforting, but as I pull on the shorts and tank top, I'm at ease.

Even though it's late, I don't go straight to sleep. Instead, I settle on the window seat to look out into the blackest night. The garden below is empty, and I stare out at the darkness wondering why my grandmother hasn't even bothered to come here to see me.

Which begs the question—what has Lycan done to my family? My father is obviously not one of his favorite people, but what could my grandmother have done? Also, the book I found earlier addressed to her has me wondering if she knew the Shaws. Perhaps Lycan's father was C.S.? I think back to the note, speaking about a wolf loving his damsel.

Can history be repeating itself?

Is that why Lycan is trying to get me to marry him?

I need to know. There are so many questions and no answers. Even though Lycan promised we would talk tomorrow, something tells me there will always be more questions, and answers may not always fulfill my need for more information.

My bare feet pad down the hallway. The sun hasn't risen yet, and even though I'd love to open the door and step out onto the patio, I have a feeling I'd be caught red-handed. Silence hangs around me, like a thick, cloying cloud, as if he's already watching. Deep down, I have a feeling Lycan knows when I make the most insignificant move. As if my breathing is on his radar. When I reach the bottom of the staircase, I turn left instead of right. I should go to the kitchen, which was my plan when I shut my bedroom door, but now that I'm here, curiosity has piqued, and my feet move voluntarily toward the office door that's currently shut.

With a gentle twist of the handle, I push open the heavy wooden panel and find myself in a dimly lit room. Stepping into Lycan's personal space feels invasive but also exciting. My stomach twists with anxiety, with fear and elation at walking in and taking something that belongs to him, just like he's taken me.

Perhaps I can find answers about what my father is hiding. Lycan promised to talk to me, to tell me the truth, but something tells me he will most certainly be keeping things he deems inappropriate from me.

All my life I've been treated like a child.

And I'm done allowing it.

Settling in the expensive leather chair, I cross my legs under my butt and pull myself closer to the heavy, wooden table, which has two drawers on either side of where I'm seated. The first one I tug on is locked, causing frustration to trickle through me. The next one slides open with ease, but all I find is a case of cigars and a stainless-steel lighter engraved with an intricate design of a wolf's head. It looks like it's howling at the moon. Underneath the etching is curled script, *The Hunt*.

Confusion furrows my brows, and I flick it open, unsure of what I'll find under the cap, but it's empty. A few streaks of black, which I'm guessing have come from the flame, but nothing more.

I open the top drawer to my left and find a small stack of envelopes and a notepad. Two sleek, silver fountain pens and a bottle of black ink. A red sealer stamp sits to the side, and once again, when I lift it, I find an engraving of a wolf's head, but this time with the name Shaw under the collar of the beast.

I continue my search, opening the last of the drawers, and find this one filled with one thick folder. Black leather etched with Shaw on the front cover, and a zipper holding everything inside.

With trembling fingers, I lift it from its hiding place and set it on the desk. The hiss of the zipper echoes in my ears, causing me to wince, praying that the sound wasn't as loud as it seemed. In the darkness, a whisper can be amplified to sound like a scream. And Lycan's hearing must be as sharp as a trained hunter because I'm certain he could hear even the slightest noise.

Flicking open the folder, I pick up the page lying on top of the stack. It's been written on the Shaw branding letterhead—a letter to my father. It's the threat he sent to Dad to get him to sign over my hand in marriage.

But as my gaze scans the words, it doesn't come across as a threat. Instead, Lycan seems to want to *save* me.

She doesn't need to know the truth to go on living and enjoying her life. You're the fuck up, not her. And I trust you'll see things my way. If you or your wife come near me or try to break the contract, I'll see to it your daughter will never speak to you again. The moment she learns of your indiscretions, she'll walk away. Think very long and hard about it, Mr. Bardot. Do you really want to lose your daughter over a stupid mistake? Unless you think your stupidity isn't an error, then I'll take Scarlett and ensure she gets the life she deserves.

Don't mistake me for a patient man. Also, do not think for one second I'm doing this for you. This is all for the girl. She will be mine, and the moment we walk out of your house, we won't return.

"Have you read enough, *fiancée*?" Lycan's deep baritone skitters across the silence toward me, the darkness swallowing his form, but his penetrating gaze is laser-sharp, and it's on me. He doesn't move from where he's leaning against the doorframe, his thick, muscled arms folded across his broad, tanned, naked chest. Even in the dim light shining through the window, I can tell this man is more Adonis than human.

"I—I…" Words escape me. My throat clogs with guilt and shame at being caught red-handed, just like all my fears coming true.

"When I promised to tell you everything in the morning, I meant it," he says, pushing away from the threshold and stepping into the room. My hungry gaze takes him in. He's only wearing a pair of red plaid sleep pants. Every other part of him is bare— feet, chest, stomach, and those arms. A memory of what happened last night trickles through my mind, and I can't stop from squirming in his chair.

He stops inches from the desk.

Dropping his hands to his sides, he pins me with a glare, and my intent stare eats up every other inch of him that was covered when he had his arms crossed. The dips and peaks of smooth skin taunt me, and the deep dip of his navel has a dark trail of hair sneaking down into the waistband of his pants.

"Are you enjoying the view, soon-to-be wife?" The amusement in his tone has me snapping my gaze to his face. Finding the corner of his mouth tipped, his green eyes blaze with intent, with malice, but also, with desire so hot it's as if a volcano has erupted behind those deep, orbs.

"I needed answers," I respond to his earlier question in an attempt not to talk about how attractive I do find him. I want to hate him right now. In this moment, I want to scream and shout, but I'd rather have him talk to me like an equal, and I know losing my shit will only have him shut down again.

"And I promised to give them to you." His expression is stern as if I'm a child who's about to get grounded for being bad. "But if you insist on acting like an insolent teenager, I'll happily lock you up and treat you accordingly."

"I just don't want to be in the dark anymore, and somehow, I don't…" Shaking my head, I push to my feet, and that's when I realize I'm wearing a tiny pair of shorts and a strappy top that fits tightly against me as if it were a second skin. Lycan's expression turns dark. His pupils widen, turning the normally green irises into black, but he doesn't smile.

"You don't?" A dark brow arches as he regards me with curious need.

"I don't trust you."

He considers this for a moment, and I almost expect him to admonish me for what I've just said, but instead, he smiles. "Good. You shouldn't."

"I'm supposed to marry you, but I can't trust you?"

Without responding, Lycan rounds the desk, stopping inches from where I'm standing. His hands land on my hips, and he holds me close, pulling me the last hairsbreadth until our bodies are flush. "I'm dangerous. I'm lethal. And I'm almost certain I will make you cry a lot more throughout this strange relationship." His brutal honesty scrapes against his throat, causing it to sound heavy, like tires on gravel.

For a long moment, I allow myself to stare at him. This close, even in the dark, he's utterly breathtaking. In such a way that I could forget how I came here. I could even push aside the fact that my father signed my life over to him. I'm still convinced he's a bastard, but he's right.

He is bad for me.

He will hurt me.

But even so, people I thought were keeping me safe all my life were clearly lying to me. The realization hits me suddenly—I'm alone. I don't have my parents to save me, which means I have to save myself.

My decision is made. I lock my gaze on his and nod. "Then allow me to learn more about the man I'm vowing to spend the rest of my life with."

LYCAN

Her request shouldn't be difficult for me, but it is. I can't deny the thought of someone knowing me inside and out scares the shit out of me because nobody has ever burrowed their way into my life, or my mind, for that matter. But those wide, cocoa irises seem to dig into me, and I allow her for a split second to see the fear bouncing around my mind before I shut down once more.

"I don't appreciate my wife snooping around my office."

"Soon-to-be wife," she throws back, a small glimmer of a smile taking hold of her plump, pink lips, which has me hungry to devour them. I could sit her on my desk. I could also spread those long, slender thighs and feast on her sweet cunt.

Temptation to do just that runs rampant through me, and I wonder what she'd do if I were to take hold of her and pin her to the smooth wooden surface and have my way with her.

Would she fight?

I would want her to. I hunger for a woman with fire to show me just how strong she is against someone like me—a beast, a wolf in an expensive suit. I step into her, my feet touching hers, the warmth of her skin burning through me.

Scarlett gently reaches for my face, her palm cupping the scruff at my jaw, sending need coursing from her tender touch to my brain. Messages of wariness hit me in the chest, but this girl, this innocent woman, can't hurt me because she'll never be able to find the one muscle in my body that would crack if I allowed it to. It has been locked away for so long I doubt it works besides the fact of keeping me alive.

"What you'll find is not something you'll be able to handle, little red," I tell her earnestly. The truth scores my esophagus, the raw honesty reminding me of just how bad I am for her.

I wanted to save her.

I wanted to claim her innocence for my own.

When her father signed the contract, I convinced myself she'd be better off with the devil than a monster. Perhaps it's because I believed her sweet light would slowly snuff out my cloying darkness.

"You don't know me very well, Lycan Shaw," she tells me, both hands holding onto my face. Her thumbs circling my stubble. Her gaze drinks me in like a fine wine, but I'm nothing of the sort. I'm a smoky whiskey at best.

I can't stop the smirk that twists on my face. I lean in, slow and steady, keeping my stare locked on Scarlett's beautiful cocoa gaze. "Trust that I'll know you by the time you say I do," I tell her. "While we stand here, at an impasse, I have the urge to bend you over my desk and spank your ass until you're screaming for me to stop. Punishment for breaking into my office and looking through my private documents."

"Then punish me," she bites, stepping back out of my hold, and my hands already miss the feel of her soft curves. Scarlett crosses her arms, her tits teasing from the low neckline of her tight top. The smooth, creamy flesh taunting from only inches away, and for a moment, I picture them bound with rope, her nipples hard and clamped while I paddle her unruly ass.

"Drop your arms." My voice is stern. There is no debate in the order, and when her eyes flash with understanding, she obeys. "Open your legs, wide." Once again, my dominant voice takes hold, the words spearing into her as she slowly shifts her bare feet on the cool, hardwood floors.

"Is that what gets you off?" Scarlett grits, her teeth grinding as her jaw ticks in frustration. Fighting the urge to chuckle, I close the distance between us and grip her shoulder. My fingers dig into the soft skin before I trail my touch down her arm to find her hip once more.

The moment I circle her waist, my hand grabs the fleshy globe of her ass, causing her to whimper when I squeeze. I know she likes the dominance. "It does. I love watching you obey me like a good little girl," I tell her.

"I'm not calling you Daddy." Her voice is cold, icy as it cools the heat between us for a second, and this time, I do laugh out loud.

"That's not my kink, sweetheart," I inform her. "But I do expect you to do as I say, in and out of the bedroom." Moving my free hand to her other hip, I hold her steady before I trace my fingers over the crack of her ass. "This is mine." My touch tickles its way over the curve of her outer thigh before I cup her between her legs. "This is mine as well."

"Lycan…" My name is a hoarse whisper that tumbles free from her lips, the usually sweet tone husky with need. "Please."

"Please?" My brow arches in question as I dip my fingers into the warm material, the wetness of her seeping through, and I feel like a god taking hold of his prize. "I like when you beg as well."

"I... I've..." Her words are mumbled, but she can't form sentences as I tease her pretty pussy with my fingers. Stroking her outside those tiny shorts, I send her reeling as her small hands grip my shoulders in a fierce hold. This is what we did in her bedroom, but this room, this space, is mine. My hand moves up, then dips under the waistband of her shorts.

"Tell me you don't want me," I order, needing her to give me permission to dip into the tight heat I know is waiting for me. "Tell me I'm a bad man, and you hate me." Her mouth opens, and for a moment, I expect her to refuse my advance, but when she doesn't, I dip two fingers into her cunt, which is dripping wet. I pump once, twice, before I lean in and whisper my lips along her cheek. "Tell me how I don't make you crave the darkness," I murmur, the warmth of my breath feathering over her neck, and my teeth latch onto the soft, fleshy earlobe, and I bite down hard, causing a slew of whimpers and moans to fall free.

"I can't." Her admission has my cock throbbing, begging to be let loose to finally claim my fiancée. I walk her back until her ass hits the desk, and I gently push her down until she's leaning back on her elbows. My hands tug at her shorts, and then they're sliding down her legs.

This is too easy.

The thought comes to me quickly, and I have a feeling my soon-to-be wife has a plan to bring this contract to an end. Only, she doesn't realize I'm the one in charge. I'm in control. She may attempt to thwart my plans, but she won't win.

I drop to one knee and push her thighs apart. Looking up at her through my lashes, I grin. "Listen to me, and listen well," I tell her before my tongue darts out to swipe at the smooth lips that glisten with arousal. Her legs tremble on either side of my face. "You can never top me from the bottom."

Her lips open into an O when I dip two fingers inside her body before I suck on her clit so hard her nails claw at the mahogany beneath her, but she can't find purchase.

"I'm in control. Always." I bite down on her clit, causing her to shake and scream out into the darkness as I devour her juices. "And when you eat, sleep, and breathe, I'll be the one making sure you do." I continue my ministrations as my mouth latches onto her smooth pussy lips, the soft hair that trails a teasing line over her mound tickles my nose. "And when this pretty little cunt comes and gushes, it will be for me, by me."

Adding a third finger, I pump faster and faster. Watching the pleasure break across her pretty face is like an adrenaline rush shooting through me. The power I have to either send her flying over the edge or keep her teetering is intoxicating.

"I wanted to save you," I admit, hoping she'll be too far gone to listen. "I wanted to make sure you weren't hurt by those closest to you, by those who promised to keep you safe, but in the end, only put you in harm's way."

Her body convulses around my fingers, and for a moment, I slow all movement, keeping her aching, trembling, and gasping for something. Her hips undulate, wanting friction against the nub of pleasure, but I hold her still.

"What are you talking about?" Scarlett breathes, her gaze glassy as she stares down at me. Her thighs still spread lewdly, her cunt dripping all over my palm. "I... Please," she pleads, realizing just how precarious her position is right now.

"I'm the one who owns you now," I tell her. "Am I understood?"

Her lips part on a squeal when I crook all three fingers, stroking the spot deep within her that has her toes curling and her fingers digging into the smooth, shiny surface beside her ass.

"I don't like to be kept waiting." The warning in my tone is gruff, darkness shrouding me as my vision turns blurry with the need to be inside her.

"Yes, sir," she mumbles before moving her hips once more to take the pleasure I'm not giving.

"Please, just allow me to come."

In all my life, no other submissive I've had kneel for me has ever pleaded so beautifully. Yes, they've been on the brink, they've begged like good little sluts, but the way Scarlett intones her words has my cock leaking against my sleep pants.

Leaning in, I suck her clit into my mouth while finger-fucking her fast and hard until the cries of her orgasm bounce off the walls of my office, and her sweet, musky essence drenches my tongue and hand. The snug, pulsing walls of her cunt squeeze my fingers, tighter and tighter, and my only thought is how she would feel around my dick.

Through my lashes, I watch her come down from the high, and it's as if she's only now realized what I've done. Admitted to certain things while keeping her high on the need to come.

I slide my fingers from her body and bring them to my mouth, licking her taste. At the sight of this, her pupils dilate further, and soon, those pretty eyes are black with lust.

"Next time you come into my office without my permission, your punishment will not be so pleasurable, little red," I tell her before rising to full height, towering over her. I help her into her shorts before I settle in my chair. "Would you like me to tell you a story?"

SCARLETT

A tale of darkness. That's what he told me, and it's been swirling in my mind even hours later as I slide under the bubbles. Warm water engulfs me, swallowing me whole, reminding me that I'm as fragile as a porcelain doll.

I listened to the story Lycan told, of how his father came to Crimson Falls all those years ago but was forced to leave. Everything he said sounded like a fairy tale gone wrong. And even though I can't imagine a little boy fleeing for his life, I realize my family isn't as innocent as I always believed.

There are secrets still hidden in Lycan's deep green eyes, and I know his admission had only been a pinch of salt in a myriad of truths. When I break the surface of the water, I open my eyes and find

Lycan leaning against the doorframe, watching me.

"I have a meeting," he tells me, but his ravenous stare drinks in my naked form. Even though he can't see much under the multitude of bubbles, my nakedness is obvious.

"Okay." I don't know why I feel disappointed in that bit of news, but I am. "I thought you were staying to tell me more." My voice takes on a tone of sadness, of frustration, which only earns me a chuckle.

"I'll be back in a couple of hours," he informs me as he pushes to full height and fills the room with his large frame. "Be a good girl, and I might even reward you tonight."

"I'm not a submissive," I throw out quickly, causing his eyes to darken at the thought.

The corner of his mouth quirks. "I beg to differ, but that's a conversation for another time and place. You're welcome to explore the house, but don't go into my office." The warning is clear. But it only piques my curiosity even more. He must know this. "I'll know every move you make," he informs me easily as if reading my mind. I watch as Lycan turns and heads for the door, throwing a look over his suited shoulder before leaving me alone to ponder what I'm going to do today.

One room I will be exploring is the library. After confirming that his father knew my grandmother,

I need to uncover more about their tryst, and I'm hoping his father had copies of the same fairy tale. I wonder if there are any more hidden notes or letters which will shed some light on their secret relationship.

Leaning back against the cool porcelain, I replay some of what Lycan told me.

"My father was a year older than your grandmother. At the time, the two names — Shaw and Bardot — were well known in Crimson Falls. They were considered royalty. And even when my dad left, there were still whispers of why and how."

Lycan's expression turns dark, and even as I snuggle into his hold, I shiver at the thought of my gran sending a man she loved away. My grandfather was strict in both personality and values, and I wonder briefly if he had forced her into marriage.

"My father loved deeply. I recall coming here when I was about five. My dad brought me here to say goodbye to the house. He told me things didn't work out but never explained why. He said there were too many ghosts, which didn't make sense to me at the time, but when I got older, when I learned the truth, I realized the ghosts weren't dead. They

were very much alive."

"So, he loved my grandmother," I whisper, wondering if that's why Lycan chose to save me. "What about my father? Did you know him after your dad sold the house? answers "

Lycan stiffens under me. "Horatio Bardot was the reason I couldn't come back to Crimson Falls for a long time. But when he walked into my club in New York, he didn't recognize me. Only later did he learn the truth, but by then, it was too late. I knew too much about him for him to ever walk away."

"But my grandmother knows you, and she knows I'm here. Isn't she angry you've taken me? Or want me to marry you?" Confusion settles in my gut like a lead weight.

Lifting my gaze, I catch sight of his nod. "She does. But she knows if she tries to stop me, she'll only hurt her family, her son. Blood is everything to Grace Bardot."

"So, she doesn't care about me."

The dark, sinister grin that curls Lycan's lips sends cold dread shooting through me. "Your grandmother knows better than to hurt another Shaw."

His gaze locks on mine before I ask, "Hurt

another Shaw? Did she hurt you in the past?"

He nods slowly, but a glimmer of rage sparkles in his eyes. "Something like that."

I push to my feet, my legs still wobbly from the orgasm he bestowed on me earlier. "I don't understand why you're treating me like a princess in your home when my family hurt yours. What did she do?"

The story seems credible. His dad loved my gran. They then went their separate ways before my dad was born. Lycan knew my father long before I ever came along. But why would he want to keep me happy, safe, if the Bardot family had broken the Shaws?

Unless they didn't.

Lycan doesn't respond, but pain etches itself on his face. An expression so agonizing it steals my breath. Realization hits me right in the chest, a confirmation of just what happened between our families.

"My father was the one who did something," I whisper, awareness creeping into my mind and tumbling from my lips. When I meet Lycan's green irises, I find agreement swirling around like a tornado about to take out anything in its path.

He promised to finish the story when he got home from his meeting. Fear skitters through my veins at the thought of having to hear the truth about my family. Never did I think my father could be anything but the good person I thought he was. I grew up believing he was a hero.

And now, I'm not so sure.

In my bedroom, I get dressed quickly, wanting to explore before Lycan returns. By the time I reach the library, I'm anxious. Not sure what I'm looking for, I start at one end of the classics shelf, slowly sliding my fingers over each spine. The fairy tales are all first editions, and I pull out every one of them.

Carrying the stack to the desk, I settle in the wingback chair and get comfortable. I pick up the top book, the gold title sparkling in the low light of the lamp that sits to my right. Flicking open Cinderella, I'm astounded to find the same scrawled handwriting on the first page, just like I did in the copy of Red Riding Hood. Confusion takes hold of me because why would the books be in Lycan's house and not my grandmother's? Surely, she would have wanted to keep them safe.

My Princess,

The clock struck midnight, and I had to leave. There wasn't a moment I didn't watch you this evening, and it was magical knowing you're mine. The gala will forever be our place. Taking you to your father's office while people danced and laughed, was nothing short of intoxicating.

I'll forever be drunk on you, my darling Grace.

One day, I will put a ring on your finger. Until then, we will forever love from afar.

Your Prince
Conall

Shutting the book, I settle back, needing a breather before I flick open the next book, finding once again a note, much like the last two I've read. Each one speaks of their love, their tryst, and their want and need for each other.

My chest tightens at the last one, where he tells her that he's leaving. It's a goodbye letter, one that drips with agony from every inked word. By the time I shut the pages, they're blurry through my tear-stained lashes.

"I thought I would bring you something to drink, Miss Bardot," Gray says as he makes his way inside carrying a tray with a cup and pot of tea. When he sets it down, I wonder briefly if he knew about my grandmother and Lycan's father.

"Thank you, Gray. Are you no longer working at my grandmother's home?" I question when I realize he should be there, not here.

He smiles. "I do. She doesn't need me today, so I'm here with Mr. Shaw." Affection graces his tone when he speaks about Lycan. He hovers for a moment before continuing, "Mr. Shaw, Lycan." A grin creases his expression as he remembers something with a faraway look on his old, wrinkled face. "He's a good boy. He didn't deserve what happened to him. His brother…" Gray shakes his head, his thoughts taking over, but his admission sending my curious nature into a spiraling tornado, and soon enough, I'm about to burst with more questions.

"His brother?" I prompt, hoping the old man can offer some answers.

He's silent for such a long moment I'm almost certain he's not going to respond, but then he focuses on my face, taking me in. "You look just like her when she was younger," he remarks, his tone wistful in remembrance. "She loved Conall so much." The sadness in his voice makes my chest ache, my heart beating wildly against my ribs.

"Are you talking about Grace? My grandmother?" Once more, I urge with a gentle push of questions, and finally, Gray nods.

"She was one of the most beautiful women to

grace this home. For years, they spent time together, falling in love, and I was convinced the curse was coming to an end."

"The curse?" I want to shoot to my feet, to grab the old man by the shoulders and shake the information out of him, but I bite down on my tongue to keep my excitement at bay. I want to know more, to learn about the affair, the relationship they had.

"There is darkness once a Bardot and a Shaw come together," Gray tells me earnestly. His voice scrapes against his throat as he admits a truth I'm sure I'm not meant to know yet. "It may be an old wives' tale," he says. "But I believe that whenever love comes between your families, something bad happens."

"Something bad?" This time I straighten, making my way to where he's standing. As if the moment is lost to him, Gray shakes his head before turning to leave. "Wait, please? What happened with my grandmother and Mr. Shaw?"

He's about to answer when the deep, rumbling baritone of my fiancé breaks through the heavy silence. "Thank you, Gray, that will be all."

The older man moves quickly, leaving me with Lycan. He doesn't seem angry as he walks toward me, unbuttoning his suit jacket before shrugging out of the sleek, black material. Left in only his light grey shirt with dark pants, he looks slightly disheveled with a tie hanging from the pocket of his slacks.

"What have you been up to, little red?" Lycan asks, his gaze tracking the books, where I've been perched for the past hour, and a bit, and the tea Gray brought for me moments earlier.

"Reading."

A dark brow arches in question as he regards me with amusement. "You're a bad liar." He steps up closer to me. "I'm sure you've discovered the stupid little love notes my father left in the books," he says. "They're useless when the person you're writing them for doesn't give a shit."

"I don't believe she didn't give a shit. Romance isn't stupid." Tilting my chin in defiance, I lock my glare on Lycan's. "And you don't know what was felt by my grandmother. Have you ever spoken to her about it? Asked her why she didn't respond?"

He considers my question before shaking his head. "I didn't need to. My father ensured she was beside him throughout their relationship, even in secret. And what did she do? She walked out and never looked back."

"How, pray tell, do you know that?"

"She married your grandfather." His words are cold. Ice cold. "That's why love is something that we can never allow between us." There's no debating this with him. His walls have been pulled up, brick by brick. He's hiding behind his anger. Instead of allowing me in, instead of talking about it, Lycan's convinced he's right.

"I will not marry a man who regards love and emotion as nonessential in a marriage."

Lycan reaches his hand into my hair, tangling his fingers in the long, dark strands before tugging me closer. "Tell me something, little red," he commands. "Do you see yourself ever loving me?"

"I don't know you." My words are spat in anger and frustration because, honestly, I haven't learned who Lycan Shaw is. Yes, he's given me some insight into his family, but I don't know him. He's made me come, he's given me pleasure, but marriage, a partnership, is not only physical. It's mental, emotional.

He leans in, his lips whispering over mine when he responds, "That's not what I asked." I half expect him to kiss me, to claim my mouth with his, but his restraint is iron-clad. "You can't love me. I'm not a man who can return emotions."

"Then why marry me?" My mind whirs with possible answers to my question. Some I don't want to think about, others make my chest ache.

But when he finally responds, it's a dark promise. "Because once you take my name, you, Miss Bardot, will carry on the Shaw legacy as it was always meant to be."

Confusion settles in my gut. My mouth opens, but I can't find the words to reply. I want nothing more than to learn about him, his family and to better understand the reasoning behind his choices. But I'm sure no matter what he tells me, no matter how much we figure out, I'll always be the girl he bought. I'm the arranged marriage he sought by blackmailing my father.

"I'm tired." I pull away from him, putting space between us as I move backward, my ass hitting the high, wooden desk. He doesn't come for me; he doesn't grab at me. I make my way past Lycan before I stop, halting my retreat, and I'm closer to the door than to him. "If you focus solely on hurting others, an eye for an eye, your life will be a series of acts that will always leave you with guilt." I move to the exit and step out into the hallway before shutting the door.

My heart cracks slightly, a barely there fissure of pain at the thought of only being here to bring children into his life. And the idea of me stuck in a loveless marriage is not what I would have envisioned for myself, but now that I'm here, perhaps I can try to fix whatever my grandmother and my father broke.

Confusion settles like a heavy weight in my gut. I don't trust Dad, not after he signed my life away, but I also can't trust Lycan. Maybe I should talk to my grandmother. Perhaps she can offer some form of truth in the swirl of bullshit I've been told over the past few days.

Tomorrow is the Bardot ball, the gala where my grandmother and Lycan's dad used to meet. Maybe, just maybe, it's time for me to expose the ugly truths of our families.

LYCAN

Shrugging on the jacket of my charcoal tux, I fasten the two buttons before straightening my tie. Usually, I'd forgo the outfit, but tonight is special. Grace will be there, and I wonder if she's going to try and stop me from marrying Scarlett. Needless to say, it won't go down well, but then again, I don't give a shit.

My fiancée needs to speak with her grandmother, which I'll allow. But once that's over and done with, she will be coming home with me. For the moment, I'll allow her to believe the story of revenge against her father, but once she bears my name, I'll gift her with the truth.

I'm the monster in our story.

Never once have I denied it. But watching

Scarlett come apart for me has made me feel like a man for the first time in a long while. She's made me *feel* something other than the need to dominate. Granted, I would devour her whole if she were to submit. And that's something I will be working on over the years we will spend together, but for now, I'm happy to play the gentleman just as long as it gets her to wear the ring, carry my name, and end her father.

With that thought in mind, I head out into the hallway, finding it silent and empty. I've become accustomed to the quiet, but I do prefer my apartment in New York, where I can keep a closer eye on Scarlett. Once this sham of a gala is over, I'll fly her out there and make sure she's under my watchful eye twenty-four seven.

When I reach Scarlett's bedroom, I push open the door without knocking. Her gasp echoes through the room, as I step into the space, taking in her slender frame in a bright red dress.

"You do realize knocking is considered polite," my feisty girl spits in frustration as she pins me with a glare so fierce it causes me to chuckle.

"This is my house, as you've learned. I make the rules." Ignoring her pursed lips, I close the distance between us. My thirsty gaze drinks her in from her perfectly painted toes to the top of her long, red hair. She doesn't flinch when I reach for her, my fingers tangling in the silky strands, and I gently tug her closer. The scent of her perfume invades my senses, and I can't stop myself from inhaling deeply, taking her fragrance in as if she were a drug, and I need to get high.

"This might be your house, and yes, you have your rules, but I still retain my privacy, as well as my need to have space from your overbearing nature," Scarlett hisses when I tighten my hold in her hair, causing glistening emotion to sparkle in her pretty eyes.

"Put your coat on. We're going to be late," I inform her, ignoring the rather arousing, yet petulant behavior of my little red. Perhaps after the gala, I'll show her exactly what my rules and her *space* entails. "I don't like to show tardiness when I'm the guest of honor."

"What?" Shock paints her pretty face, but I don't respond. Instead, I make my way to the door, leaning against the frame as I wait for her to pull on the crimson coat that matches her dress. There's a hood, which will come in handy since it's chilly outside.

She joins me with no more questions. Side by side, we look like a couple, and I know most of the guests tonight will want to know how the wedding plans are going. I'm almost certain her grandmother has warned the guests not to attend, but I have more pull around here, and I will make sure it's the event is the talk of the town.

The moment we reach the landing, my phone buzzes in my pocket. A call from Kahn. "Yes?"

"I have a problem." His icy tone is filled with frustration. I sent him and his team to look for my brother, but we also have Lorenzo to deal with. Everything is happening at the same time, and for a moment, I wonder if there's a connection. I'm not sure why I would even consider this, but the coincidence is too obvious.

"If it's my brother, kill him. If it's Lorenzo, let's call Alex and see if we can move in on the church," I respond, glancing at my fiancée to find her staring, wide-eyed at me.

"Lorenzo has gone underground. I have an inkling on where, but we raided the church and found nothing of consequence. That's not something you would want to tell Alexei." He's right. Going back to the mafia boss to tell him I lost the bastard he's looking for will only be a confirmation that we're not able to tackle a job so insignificant.

"Where was the last place he was spotted?"

"New Mexico," Kahn tells me, and I have a feeling we may need help from the Cartel, which means calling Victor Cordero, and that's not a man I want to be involved unless we need him.

"I'm headed to the gala right now. It's

important." I don't need to explain. Kahn knows why I have to be there. "Get the jet ready. I'll fly out tonight and make sure the apartment is ready for Scarlett. She'll be joining me."

"Yes, boss."

Once I hang up, I turn to a stunned beauty who's glaring at me as if I've grown a second head in the time of my phone call. "I'll have the maid pack some clothes. We're leaving after the gala."

"Where? I can't just leave."

"New York. And you will do whatever I say. There are secrets in the city that may offer you the answers you're seeking." It's not entirely a lie, but it's also not the whole truth. Yes, there are answers in the Big Apple that Scarlett would need to learn about, but it may have to wait until after the wedding.

"This is ridiculous. I can stay with my grandmother. I don't need to follow you around like a lost puppy." Her adamant tone has anger surging through me. She doesn't realize just how much I'm doing for her, and perhaps that's the problem. Maybe I should offer her more answers, just to ensure she's on my side.

"Listen to me," I say, turning to face her fully. My hands cupping her smooth, tanned cheeks. "Your father has secrets in New York, things he's been hiding for years. I cannot tell you about them, or I'll break the contract—"

"You mean that if you were the one to divulge the secrets, I wouldn't have to marry you." Such an intelligent girl. "Is that why you want to keep me in the dark? I could just go to my grandmother and ask her about it. She'd tell me the truth."

"Would she?" I challenge easily, knowing that Grace Bardot would rather die than tell her sweet granddaughter about her past and present secrets.

For a long moment, Scarlett stares at me. Her lips part on a soft sigh before she shakes her head. "I don't know." There's a sadness to her face, an emotion I want to eradicate.

Stepping closer to her, eating up the distance between us, I allow my larger frame to loom over her. With my index finger under her chin, I tilt her head until she's looking directly at me. The silence hangs heavy with desire. As much as Scarlett doesn't *want* to feel something, she knows there's a magnetism between us, it's palpable.

"I want nothing more than to keep you here tonight, to sit with you on the couch, drink whisky, and talk about growing up as a Shaw." My admission is startling to both of us, but I don't stop. "I want you to know who I am. Even though I'm the monster in this story, the wolf seeking out his prey, I wouldn't hurt you. Not unless you want it."

"You'd just devour me whole until nothing is left," Scarlett responds, the confession true as it escapes her glossy lips.

Arching a brow at her, I challenge, "I didn't hear you complaining the last time I made you come."

The corner of her mouth quirks. "No, you're right. I want to hate you—"

"But you can't. It's not who you are." It's true. The woman before me may have anger toward me for what I did, but she doesn't hate. It's not in her vocabulary. Not in her personality. And as much as I wish I could remain cold-hearted where Scarlett is concerned, I can't deny the pull, the desire that warms my blood each time she's near.

Call it lust.

Call it stupidity.

But it's most definitely undeniable.

SCARLETT

I didn't think I would find myself intrigued by Lycan. Or grow to want to know more about him, but over the past couple of weeks, I have. It feels as if I've been here for months already. Instead, it's not been that long at all. As we near the Bardot house, Lycan offers me his arm, which I accept.

I wanted to bring him down. But I have a feeling there's so much more to this story than I wanted to admit. There are secrets he's keeping from me, and the more time I spend with him, I'm almost certain I can learn the truth about my family.

The admission Gray offered about the curse has also been playing on my mind. I'll ask Grace what happened with Conall; she has to tell me. I'm her blood. Her family. She cannot refuse me answers when I'm about to walk down the aisle with the son of her first love.

The door stands open, golden light flowing from the entrance, and we're welcomed by one of the servants I recognize from when I arrived. Seconds after our coats are taken, we're escorted through the living room entrance where a few guests are already mingling.

"There she is." Grace's voice comes from behind me, and I turn to find my grandmother looking as elegant as ever. "Darling, you look beautiful." She leans in, gripping my shoulders and places a kiss on each of my cheeks. When her gaze lands on the man beside me, I notice a flicker of annoyance, but other than that, my grandmother is a steel mask of happiness. "Lycan," she grits but smiles as she does it. Shocking me, my grandmother takes his hands, leaving me to gawk at them. "I trust you're well. It's been far too long."

A cruel smirk curls Lycan's lips, and I'm sure he's about to insult her in some way, but he says, "Likewise, Mrs. Bardot." I realize my soon-to-be husband is playing a role. "I think once the party is underway, we should have a chat. There are a few things I need to go over with you." It's not a friendly request; it's an ice-cold command.

"I have company, Lycan." All my life, knowing my grandmother, I've never seen her falter, but right

211

now, she's shaking as her throat works on a nervous swallow.

As much as I want Lycan to drop it, I have a feeling he's only going to continue on his quest until she agrees. And I'm not wrong, but also shocked when he says, "I'm hoping to take Scarlett to the Big Apple tomorrow, so what we need to talk about has to be tonight."

"Oh!" A gasp from my gran is the only expression of shock to his words. "Are you sure you should be traveling to the city this week?"

"There's no need to worry. I'll take care of her," he assures my grandmother, who seems even more uncomfortable now than she was moments ago.

Her gaze locks on mine, and she offers a grin. "You'll absolutely love it." My grandmother says before she's dragged away to other guests. I attempt to appear normal while my life feels like it's falling apart before my very eyes.

"Close your mouth, little red," Lycan whispers in my ear. "The only time I want that mouth parted in an O is when my dick is about to slide between those lips." His words are filled with amusement, but I don't laugh.

"What is happening? Why does she not want us traveling to New York? What are you not telling me? She seemed almost scared to refuse your request to talk to her. Why?" My questions are drenched in curiosity as a hiss of frustrated breath escapes my lips.

Lycan's green eyes sparkle with indignation as if he's angry that I'm even asking him about his relationship with my family, with my grandmother. His hand reaches for my arm. Taking me by the elbow, he leads me away from the crowd down a long, darkened hallway until we reach an office where he shoves me inside and kicks the door shut behind him.

"If you want to be punished, little red, I'll gladly oblige," he informs me as his hands grip the thick leather of his belt. Thoughts of him spanking me, whipping me until I'm begging for more, invade my mind, and I'm squirming on the spot.

"Don't change the subject," I bite out, crossing my arms in front of my chest after tugging myself free of his hold. "I want to know the truth. I'm done staying in the dark."

"I thought you liked the darkness, little red?" Lycan challenges as he moves closer to me, eating up the distance I've put between us in two long strides. As much as I want to run, I don't. I tilt my chin in defiance.

"We better get back to the party before my grandmother looks for us," I tell him, ignoring his question because if I had to be honest, I would say yes. I do enjoy the darkness. I want more of it, but

213

right now, I want answers.

"You didn't answer my question. I don't like repeating myself," he informs me. "That calls for a harsh punishment." A fire blazes in his eyes as he steps into my personal space, his hands gripping my elbows as he holds me steady. There's no running from Lycan, not right now. "And tonight, I'll show you just what kind of punishment comes from you not answering me when I question you."

"Then do it," I bite out as frustration claws its way up my throat. "Why don't you do it right now?" I challenge, hoping he'll quell the ache that's started twisting in my gut. I may have denied the fact that I'm submissive to him, but it was a lie. Right now, all I want is for him to bend me over right here on the arm of the sofa and spank me.

I don't have to wait long before Lycan spins me around, hitches my dress over my hips, and one of his large hands comes down on my ass with a loud swat. A squeal of surprise tumbles from my lips, and another spank lands on the other cheek. He continues my punishment with grunts and growls rumbling in his chest. And my lips expel moans of pleasure with each smarting swat.

By the time I'm trembling, he stops. I don't know how many times his hand landed on my behind, but the sting is apparent. I'm certain my ass is bright red. Lycan's fierce grip in my long tresses tugs me to stand, and the hemline of my dress slinks down my thighs, hiding my panty-clad butt.

"Next time, it will be my belt," he promises along my neck before his teeth graze the lobe of my ear along with the threat. "Now, let's go out there and look like a happily engaged couple."

He takes my hand and leads me out into the throng of the party, where guests are drinking, chatting, and laughing. Music tinkles from the speakers as we move through the crowd and into the dining room, leading out onto the patio. Similar to Lycan's home, this one is illuminated with fairy lights that twinkle around pillars.

"It's scary how alike your house is to my grandmother's," I remark as we stop at the bar where Lycan orders me a white wine, and he gets himself a whiskey.

"It's the reason they built them, the ancestors of our families." A new tidbit of information I had no clue about. It seems every day with him, I'm learning something new. Lycan leans in his hot breath at my ear. "I bet that sweet cunt is soaked for me right now. Even with all these people around, you're needy for me to make you come again. Aren't you, little red?"

A gasp of surprise expels from my lungs at his salacious taunt, but I can't deny it, so instead of answering, I sip my drink. With our glasses in hand, we greet a few guests. Some I recognize as celebrities

215

or famous politicians. Others are strangers to me. But it seems Lycan knows a lot more people here than I thought he would.

When the dinner bell rings, we move to the long table that's been set with the most expensive china and the shiniest cutlery. I slip into a seat near the far end of the table from where my grandmother sits, and Lycan settles in beside me.

The staff brings out plates of steaming food, but I can't concentrate when a looming figure slips into the chair to my right. Beside me, Lycan stills, his body turning rigid, and his knuckles turn white as he grips his knife so tight I'm half expecting it to shatter.

"What are you doing here?" His voice is laced with poison as if his words could kill the man beside me. When I turn my head, glancing up at the intruder, I'm shocked to see hazel eyes looking back at me.

"Brother," the man says, and that's when it hits me. This is Lycan's brother. The man who chased me through the woods, scaring me into his brother's arms, sealing my fate without knowing it. "I don't think you want to cause a scene," he says, glancing past me toward Lycan. "But I wanted to say hello to your pretty new fiancée."

"It's best that you walk out before I kill you."

"Always with the theatrics." A chuckle vibrates

in his throat. With everyone's focus on dinner, nobody has noticed the interaction at this end of the table. But when I glance to my left, I find my grandmother watching intently, her knife and fork poised, waiting for a war I'm sure will soon be here.

"Darius." The name is a warning, causing my gaze to land back on Lycan. "If you even dare touch her, I will end you." There is no humor in his tone, and I don't doubt he's capable of killing someone. Something about his demeanor tells me he's done it before. And that sends an icy shrill of dread racing through me.

"Let's enjoy dinner," Darius says. "I'll be leaving shortly after. Also, I wanted to tell you face-to-face, call your bloodhounds off me, or I will *end them* one by one."

I feel like I'm watching a tennis match. Left to right, the threats are thrown, and I wonder who will give in first. I doubt it will be Lycan. He's a man who gets what he wants, and no doubt he will spill blood to do it.

"If I weren't convinced you are a threat, I would," Lycan responds before gulping down his drink and signaling for another. I take my own glass and swallow back the wine. I'm caught between feuding brothers.

A dangerous place to be.

LYCAN

He's so close, yet so far.

If I did anything to him now, I'll fuck up my chances of business with every man in this room. As much as they may be corrupt, they won't allow first-hand violence into their lives.

And Darius knows it.

But what bothers me more is that he's seated beside Scarlett. Jealousy surges through me, along with rage and the need to kill. My brother was nothing more than a two-faced bastard who ran before he even realized what had happened to our father.

His beard is longer than I remember, his eyes darker, filled with what I can only imagine are more sinister intentions. He glances at Scarlett, interest sparking in his gaze, and I wonder what he's really doing here.

He's not a fan of the Bardots either. Since we were little, we knew about the old woman who lived next door, but when we learned about her connection with our father, something in us changed. We knew we would never be close to the family.

And I'm sure now that I'm marrying Scarlett, Darius is fuming. As dinner is served, Scarlett's hand finds my thigh, causing me to clank my knife and fork against the fine china plate, ensuring every pair of eyes are on me.

Once the conversation starts up again, I glance at my girl, whose eyes are wide as she regards me. She leans in close, her lips inches from my ear, which doesn't help my need for her. "I think perhaps we should leave early," she tells me with a soft kiss to my earlobe, and my zipper is suddenly much tighter than it was moments ago.

"If you keep that up, you're going to have trouble on your hands," I tell her.

A soft giggle falls from her lips, and I want to steal every whimper she makes. But right now, we need to behave. There are people here I need to impress. Most times, I don't give a shit about who's watching; other times, I quite like an audience, but for now, I know Scarlett's reputation means more than me getting my rocks off.

"Eat your dinner, and when you're done, we'll leave." My voice is low, a whisper only Scarlett can hear. I pray to all that's holy she obeys.

With a slight nod, she eats, and I smile, watching her enjoy the dinner. My appetite is gone, or rather, it's shifted from my plate to the woman beside me. Lifting my gaze, I find Darius staring at me.

"Still in control," he remarks, but I don't respond because if I do, it will start a war. And that's not what I want or need right now. "You can hate me all you want," he tells me, talking over Scarlett who's between us. The only sweetness amongst the darkness that's lingering in the room. My brother and I are far too similar, and even though I don't consider him family, or at least close family anymore, he is blood.

Blood is a bitter vow to swallow. The lingering metallic flavor of guilt and deception hangs between us, and I know it will never be cleaned. It will never change.

I turn my attention to my drink, swallowing back the biting bourbon, allowing the burn to trickle down my throat until the fire has reached my stomach. My gut churns with the need to escape.

"You know, little one," Darius says, his voice loud enough for only me and Scarlett to hear. "He's never going to love you like you want. Marrying him may be your end." There's no joking in his tone, but I didn't expect there to be.

"I may one day grow old beside him, and maybe I don't love him yet, and he may not feel the same for me, but I'm not ever going to regret doing this. My life is my own. Even if I'm under contract, Lycan has given me a choice to walk away…" She glances at me before looking back at Darius. "But I don't want to." Her final words to him have my chest tightening as emotions I don't want or need take hold of me, and I'm soon lost in affection for the girl beside me, the same girl I bought from her father.

Affection is weakness, but I can't stop myself when it comes to her. Scarlett does something to me. She knocks down walls, breaks through steel doors, and burrows herself in the darkness I've long since buried.

Darius doesn't say anything, but the look he gives me tells me everything I need to know—he's impressed with Scarlett.

And that can never be a good thing.

SCARLETT

My nerves are shot. With Darius here, I know he's only trying to goad Lycan to act out, but the man who's now standing beside me is far too controlled, and I'm certain his brother knows that.

A stunning woman sidles up beside Lycan, so close I can smell her perfume. He stills beside me. His body turns rigid as he grips me tighter but doesn't say anything. She moves past us, and I notice the sway of her hips and the way her long hair hangs in silky waves down her back. She casts a quick glance over her shoulder at my fiancé before she disappears amongst the rest of the guests.

His arm snakes around my waist even tighter, and I find it difficult to breathe as we head toward my gran to say goodbye. I find her eyes on me, watching, intrigued by us. And I wonder if she'll tell my father about Lycan's display. Lycan grabs a flute of champagne, handing it to me before he orders a scotch from the waiter who scurries off to get the drink.

When I sip on the bubbly liquid, I pray the alcohol will calm the erratic thumping of my heart and the flurry in my belly. I want to come across as confident, calm, but with the man beside me who draws every woman's eye, I feel like a teenager beside him.

"Can I have your attention, please?" My grandmother calls out, clinking her glass with a silver knife. As the crowd falls silent, she continues, "Tonight is a very special one for the Bardot family.

It's a night I didn't think would ever come to pass." Her eyes land on Lycan and me before she speaks, "But I'm so happy to finally say that my granddaughter, Scarlett Bardot, is engaged."

A flurry of murmurs fills the room after her announcement, and my cheeks heat as every set of eyes turn toward us. The strange, yet elegant woman who seems to focus on Lycan stares at him for a long moment before she turns her attention to me. Rage burns in the stare she pins on me, before she flicks her hair and rushes to the patio but doesn't walk outside. She lingers in the doorway, and I notice her opening her purse.

"Who is she?" I whisper as I attempt to smile at my grandmother who's embarrassing me more than I've ever been before.

"She's nobody," Lycan assures me under his breath, but I know it's a lie. Nobody can ever be nothing to another person when they act like that. The jealousy is clear. There's no doubt about it, that woman and Lycan were involved, and it was more serious than he's letting on.

"Let *me* make something clear," I hiss as my grandmother continues. "Never lie to me again." I step forward as my gran calls me over, and I make my way toward her, stopping beside her as she gifts me a show of affection.

LYCAN

Fire courses through my veins. The need to pin her down and whip her with my belt has taken over, but I can't do shit since her grandmother is standing a few feet away. As much as I don't mind an audience, that would be pushing my nonexistent limits.

When Scarlett joins me again after her grandmother allows her to, I wrap my arm around the slender waist of my pretty little red and tug her into my hold. The movement earns me a soft gasp of surprise. There are eyes on us, waiting to see what I'll do. With a slow smirk crawling along my lips, I turn to Scarlett, cupping her face in my free hand, and pull her closer, touching my lips to hers.

Every set of eyes that are watching us scorches

224

my skin. I know there is one woman who is ready to kill, who will easily take Scarlett from me, but I can't let that happen, so when my beautiful bride-to-be opens her mouth, I allow my tongue to dive into her sweetness and put on the show everyone was waiting for.

A cheer surrounds us, clapping and shouting, a few pats on my back as I pull away from Scarlett, and I smile at the viper who's piercing me with her glare. I can't help but taunt her with a tip of my head, knowing that I'm goading her into making a fool of herself. She spins on her heel, leaving the room and heading outside, and I watch for a short moment as she lights up one of her long, menthol cigarettes. The shit used to stink up my bedroom, but when I let her go, I made sure to never come close to falling down that dark abyss again.

The guests congratulate us, but my mind is on getting out of here, making sure I can leave with Scarlett as soon as possible. The jet is ready, and I'm aching to be on it, with the woman in my arms, as we fly to New York. Heaven is waiting for me, and we'll leave the devils behind.

It should be easier to fake a smile. Especially with the assholes in this room, but deep down, I don't want to. I'm exhausted. Playing a game I know I'm no longer focused on. Each of the men at the party are clients of my club, and they all know what goes on in those private rooms.

Music tinkles from the band that's been set up in the corner of the large ballroom. People couple up around us, as the party properly gets underway. They dance and sway along the space that's been turned into a dance floor, and I decide it's time to escape.

"Let's go." I take Scarlett's hand and lead her to where Grace is standing, talking to guests I don't recognize. Her gaze turns to us as we near her, and the glint of annoyance in her expression makes me smile. "Thank you for a lovely evening, but Scarlett and I have to leave. I have business I need to finish up before we get to the jet."

"Oh," she gasps. "I'm sorry to see you go," she tells her granddaughter, not meeting my stare. "We'll need to talk. I hope you can give me a call soon. There are so many things I'd like to catch up with you on."

"We'll be back soon," Scarlett tells her grandmother. "I would like to talk to you about the books." I tense when Scarlett mentions those, and I notice her grandmother's mouth pinch in frustration before she looks at me. "I found them, I mean, those notes."

"We need to leave," I speak up, knowing that this is not the time and place to get into this fucking conversation. "Thank you again, Grace. It was lovely as usual." My hand in Scarlett's tightens, and I offer her a squeeze of warning as I take a step away.

"Darling, please," Grace pleads in a hushed whisper before we can escape. "Leave the past where it is," she informs Scarlett. "It's no longer relevant. Move on."

Tension bunches my muscles, holding tight as they twist. I know she'll never tell Scarlett the truth, that she walked away from the only man who loved her just to marry a piece of trash, gold-digging bastard. I'm sure there's more to the story, but because my father is dead and all his secrets buried with him, I doubt I'll ever find out.

"Why are you being this way?" Scarlett's plea hits me square in the chest. Her words so soft, whispered with such pained tenderness, even my breath is stolen from my lungs. I've never been aware of women, never allowed their tears to burden me. I quite enjoyed them crying, pleading for mercy. But there's something about the way my little red speaks to her grandmother that does shit to me. Shit, I don't need to be feeling.

It's dangerous.

When I came to the agreement with Horatio, I knew Scarlett would color my monochrome world, but never did I think she'd make me *feel*. Shaking my head, I step between the women.

"It's time to go, Scarlett." I pull her into the

crook of my arm. "We'll be back to see Grace again soon." I allow the hint of warning to lace my words as I meet the old woman's gaze. The shimmering of guilt dances in her stare, but I don't want to question just what the fuck she's hiding. The sooner we can get out of here, the better.

I tug Scarlett beside me as we make our way to the exit. The large door carved from heavy, dark wood opens and allows us to leave the warmth of the house. But instead of turning for the car, which I note Gray is waiting inside the driver's seat, I veer off in the opposite direction.

"Where are we going? I thought we were going home?" Scarlett's use of the word home makes my mouth curl into pure satisfaction.

Could this be her acceptance of her position beside me?

Of our upcoming wedding?

"We're going to take the scenic route home," I tell her while leading her through the vast, manicured garden, which greets us with the dimly lit shadows that dance across the grass.

When we reach the entrance to the woods, Scarlett stops dead in her tracks, causing me to turn. Her eyes are wide, fear flitting through those pretty orbs, gems that sparkle with unbridled darkness.

"We're going through there?" Her question

comes out in a soft, fearful whisper, her lips parting into a dick-hardening O. I want nothing more than to show her just how much I love that little expression on her face, but I'll wait until we're swallowed by the murkiness of the trees.

"Yes." It's one word, an order, no debating, and my little red sees it. She knows when I use my commanding, Dominant voice to never question me. With a slight nod, she steps up to me, and we slink in between the trees. I know the path like the back of my hand.

But she doesn't.

And that's what makes this so much fun.

A gentle tremble skitters through her, and my arm tightens around her small frame.

"I know you like the darkness," I say, knowing she can't *not* hear me right now. It's as if we're the only two people in the world. We walk in relative silence as we move deeper into the woods.

Thick branches hide us from any prying eyes. I stop halfway to the house and tug her against me. Leaning back against the thick, wooden trunk of a tree, I stare down into her eyes that are glinting from the shards of silver peeking through the trees from the moon above.

"Would you like to please me?" I ask, lowering the commanding tone to a hushed whisper. But the bite of dominance still lingers.

For a moment, she considers her response. I watch as emotions dance across her pretty features. I'm almost certain she's about to say no, to refuse, when she shocks me and smiles. "I would like to please you," she whispers.

My hands land on her shoulders, and I push her down to her knees. The moment she hits the ground, my cock thickens, throbbing against my zipper as if trying to escape the confines. "Then you will have to learn to take me into that pretty little throat of yours, little red," I inform her with a low rumble.

Scarlett reaches for my belt with trembling hands, her fingers deftly moving to undo the buckle with a clinking echo. The hiss of my zipper is loud in the silence that surrounds us, and soon, her soft, gentle touch has me grinding my teeth, my eyes shut tight as I try not to come like a fucking teenager who's never been touched before.

Her movements are slow, almost unsure, but when I open my eyes and watch her tongue dart out to lick the arousal at my tip, my balls tighten with the threat of spilling my seed all over her pretty face.

Fisting my hands at my sides, I stare down as Scarlett takes me into her mouth and her warmth envelops me, making every nerve in my body spark with desire and need to use her like a fuck doll for my pleasure.

Her plump lips slide down the shaft as she

swallows me deeper into her heat, the tightness of her throat pulsing around the tip, and her gag reflex takes hold. A cough and splutter from her lips only wets my dick with her saliva, making the in-and-out slide easier.

With one hand, I grip her long, red tresses in my fist and control her movements, making sure to hit the back of her throat each time. And every time I do, she chokes on my cock.

"Breathe through your nose, little red," I tell her through gritted teeth as I slide out and thrust back in. The shimmering tears from her lashes sparkle in the dim light, making her look like a beautiful toy only made for my amusement and pleasure.

I'm sure her knees are protesting against the hard ground, but she doesn't fight it, she doesn't squirm. Without order, she binds her hands behind her back and allows me all the control I need to fuck her mouth like I would her pretty cunt.

The image of her bound in Shibari rope sparks in my mind, dancing like a movie scene, and my cock throbs at the picture. Using my hold on her, I pull her head back, then force it forward until I feel her throat constrict around my shaft, spit drips down her chin onto the elegant dress she wore tonight.

It's ruined.

And I know the moment I find my release, she'll be ruined too.

SCARLETT

Watching Lycan in control is like watching a king rule over his kingdom. I can't help but be in awe of just how much he possesses me when we're like this. If it's not his hands making me feel like I have to please him, making me wet and needy, it's his cock.

He thrusts into my mouth, making me gag. He smiles when the saliva soaks my dress. His thickness makes my jaw ache, but seeing the pleasure written on his face only seems to have an effect on me I never thought possible.

I'm turned on.

I'm pleased that I'm giving him pleasure.

Perhaps, underneath it all, I am submissive.

He uses me like I'm nothing more than a rag

doll. His cock thickens, choking me as he pumps once, twice, and on the third and final thrust, his warm seed spills over my tongue, and I quickly swallow his flavor. And I find even though I want to hate it, hate him, I don't. The salty sweetness of his release is enjoyable.

Lycan slowly pulls from my mouth, and I watch, still on my knees, how he guides his cock into his pants and zips himself up. He silently helps me to my feet and brushes off my dress before straightening and meeting my gaze.

I don't have time to speak because his mouth crashes against mine, his tongue stealing itself inside my mouth as he devours me, and I'm certain tasting himself on my tongue. The kiss is breathtaking, possessive, and I find my hands twining around his neck as I pull him closer.

And to say my panties are now soaked would be a gross understatement. He's done something to me, broken through the walls, shattered the glass cage I'd built around me, and now amongst the shards, he's stolen me from the forest and captured more than just my body. He's taken my mind.

But he can't have my heart, I remind myself.

By the time we land in New York, I'm exhausted.

I'm not sure what time it is, but I do know it's early morning because the sun hasn't risen yet. In the dark, we make our way to the waiting town car. Lycan slips into the back seat with me and orders the driver to take us to Hawthorne.

Lycan's hand is on my thigh, the confidence and demanding way he holds onto me confirms I'm his now. What we did in the woods still lingers in my mind, and it's as if his taste is now forever on my tongue. I've never found pleasure in doing that with a guy, not even the boys I dated before my life changed forever. But with Lycan, I felt like a queen, even though I was on my knees.

Lycan squeezes my thigh, causing me to turn my attention toward him. His gaze holds mine hostage with promises I can't fathom. I asked him to show me his world, and I have a feeling I'm about to walk into the wolf's den.

But I'm not afraid.

Not anymore.

I thought I would be. I figured the moment I'm alone with him, I would want to run and hide, but he makes me feel strong. It's strange, as if his strength and confidence courses through me as well.

"Stop thinking so much," Lycan tells me with a grin. "I can hear that pretty mind racing beside me." The amusement in his tone makes me blush. I don't want to feel child-like next to him, but there are times my inexperience shines like a beacon in the night.

"This world you're about to show me," I start, "it's new to me. So new, in fact, that I'm scared I won't fit in." My admission has his free hand reaching for one of mine.

"Trust me, little red," he tells me. "You fit in perfectly. Your sweetness, that innocence that shines like a star in the night sky, and your delicious submission."

"But I never—"

"You did. What do you think happened in the woods? The fact that you happily kneeled before me and took my cock in your mouth, that's what I crave. Watching you douse your fire just a little bit to please me," he speaks, his voice laced with desire, before he leans in and brushes his lips along my cheek. "That was what a perfect submissive would do—anything to please her Dominant."

"So, I'm going to need a safe word?" The question is a mere whisper, one that makes my stomach twist and churn with nervous energy.

Lycan chuckles. "You will. Since you're to be my wife, I wanted to take this slowly. Most women I've been with were only there for a night. And most of them were used to this world already. With you, I needed to savor watching you slowly find your submission. I wanted you to discover it naturally, not by force."

"I thought—"

"When you're unsure, ask. Don't think about things you've never witnessed." Lycan assures me with a smile as he leans in closer, his mouth at my ear, the warm breath fanning over my cheek when he whispers, "But trust me, little red, when we play, I'll make sure the desires you have, those dark, twisted needs, will be fulfilled. And when I do pin you down and take your pussy for the first time, you'll scream."

The promise, the dark, lust-filled vow he offers me, sends heat coursing through my veins like fire through the woods. I want to speak, to respond, but I can't find the words. Thankfully, the car comes to a stop. My head whips to my left to find my new home for the next few days. Lycan's New York home is nothing like I expected.

I figured someone like him would have a bachelor pad in the city, but we're in the suburbs. The house before us is a three-story mansion with soft yellow lights that shimmer from only the lower windows.

"I thought we were going to your apartment in the city?" I ask as I take in the house through the window. The two large white pillars holding up the balcony on the second floor have vines snaking around them, and the open-brick façade is nothing short of magnificent. Lycan's driver opens my door and helps me out of the car. The gravel beneath my feet crunches when I step on it.

"I wanted you to see our future home on the West Coast," Lycan says when he joins me, his hand clasping mine as we head toward the double wooden doors that slide open as if knowing their master is home. The foyer is filled with soft light. Dark metal railings lead up a sweeping staircase, and large modern paintings hang on the walls as they disappear down the hallway toward the right.

The scent of food wafts toward us. "This is magnificent," I say as Lycan leads me toward the back of the house and into the enormous kitchen. Stainless steel and marble greet us as I take in the space. A countertop is filled with fresh bread and baked goods.

"Master Shaw," a man in chef's whites greets before his gaze lands on me. "Good evening, miss." The posh British accent is clear in his words, and a soft smile curls his lips. "It's lovely to have you both here."

"Thank you," I respond, a grin forming on my face.

"Marcel, this is Scarlett. She'll be spending some time here while I attend my meetings this week," Lycan informs the man whose smile widens as he regards me.

"It's lovely to meet you, Miss Scarlett," Marcel says. "I'll happily keep you company while you're visiting at Hawthorne."

"We'll see you in the morning," Lycan says before tugging me behind him before I have a moment to answer Marcel's kindness. I'm taken back into the foyer before we head up the stairs, my gaze flitting between artworks as we move down the hall. We stop outside a dark wooden door, and I watch as Lycan unlocks it with a brass key and twists the handle. He allows me to enter first.

The room is furnished in blacks, whites, and grays. There are no other colors anywhere in sight. The bed is draped in a black comforter, matching pillows, and the four posters are made of a dark wood.

The carpet underfoot is a soft, plush charcoal, and the curtains, in a slate hue, are lined, blocking out any threat of light. A shimmering softness beckons, and I walk over to touch the silky material.

"You'll sleep in here tonight. I haven't had your room made up yet," Lycan speaks softly, causing me to turn and regard him, only to find him unbuttoning his shirt. The motion makes my cheeks heat, and my stomach somersaults at the thought of finally seeing him naked.

Shaking my head, I respond in an attempt to quell the need in my gut. "I don't need to have a room made up. I'm happy to just take any room."

"This isn't a debate, little red," Lycan tells me in a no-nonsense tone.

Folding my arms across my chest, I pin Lycan with a glare, but I only earn myself a chuckle of amusement in response. "I may have enjoyed what we did in the forest, but—"

He closes the distance between us in no time before he stops, looming over me. "What did we do in the forest, sweetheart?" he growls, the sound so feral it's as if the beast has come out to play. The flames dancing in his eyes send a shudder of warmth over me, making everything south of my belly button tingle with anticipation. When I don't respond immediately, he leans in. "I asked you a question."

"I... We... I mean, you know what we did," I bite out, frustration at my nervousness around him, causing me more annoyance than anything else.

"Oh? Why don't you remind me?" The challenge is evident in his voice, in his expression of interest, which he holds me hostage with. This close, Lycan is handsome, devilishly so with a wolfish smirk that makes my stomach flutter with excitement.

"Stop acting like a domineering asshole," I bite out through clenched teeth in an attempt to steer us off the conversation because as much I want to say it, I can't bring myself to talk dirty to him.

The corner of his mouth quirks. "Does my little red not like being a filthy girl for me?" he taunts as he reaches for my chin, holding it between his thumb and forefinger as he holds me steady so I can't look away from him. I can't turn my gaze from the man who's staring at me as if he's trying to see into my soul.

Swallowing the lump in my throat, I whisper, "I sucked your cock."

Fire blazes in Lycan's eyes, the color turning molten, sending heat scorching through me at my filthy words. I'm sure he's heard worse, heard dirtier, but for me, this is new. "Good girl," he praises. "And would you like me to pleasure you now?" He tips his head to the side while still holding onto my chin. "Would you like me to devour your pretty cunt until you're gushing all over my face and tongue, little red?"

"I..." Words fail me. I knew Lycan wouldn't be like any guy I've ever been with in the past, but his mouth is pure filth. "I'm not sure."

A rumble vibrates in his chest. "I think you do. I think your mind is whirling with images of my face between your legs. You do realize I've been hungry for you since the moment I saw you. I wanted to taste you since the moment you walked into your parents' dining room that night."

My mouth gapes at his confession. "You didn't

even know me."

"I knew I wanted you; that was more than enough." There's no doubt in his words, no doubt in his eyes, and I have a feeling he knew I would eventually submit to this thing between us. Not the marriage, not the heavy ring on my finger, but the fact that my body craves his. Not only his touch, but so much more than that.

"Then do it."

Lycan moves swiftly, his free hand tangling in my long hair. He tugs my head back painfully, exposing my throat to his mouth. Lips and teeth attack me like a hungry beast as he kisses, sucks, and bites at my sensitive flesh.

"Once I'm inside you, little red, there is no running," Lycan warns in a low murmur along the column of my neck. "And when you come around my cock, my tongue, and my fingers, no other man will ever enter you. Are we clear?"

I nod because I can't find words. I'm lost to the pleasure rocketing through me as Lycan bites down on the smooth skin, and I know there'll be a bruise left after his attack. He releases me, allowing both hands to slide down my body until he's cupping my ass through the dress I'm still wearing. Lifting me against him, he walks us to the bed before throwing me to the soft mattress.

"Tonight, I'm going to have you, claim you, and

when I'm done, that ring will forever be attached to your finger," he commands as he shifts the material of his shirt over his shoulders. The broad, muscled expanse of tanned flesh greets me with a taunt because I can't reach him. My fingertips tingle with the need to touch, to feel, to run along every dip and peak of his beautifully toned body.

A dark smattering of hair between the pecs of his chest makes me think about how it would feel against my breasts. Lowering my gaze to his stomach, I take in the dips of his abs, as well as the angled muscles that dip into the waistband of his dark slacks.

A trail of black hair sneaks down, trailing under the material toward his thickening erection. When my gaze snaps back to Lycan's, I find him smirking down at me.

"Enjoying the view, little red?" A dark brow arches in question, his challenge clear. He knows what he does to me. Confidence oozes from him like a cologne, and it engulfs me, holding me hostage in the masculine scent of him.

"Perhaps," I tease, my hands moving to my dress as I tug the hem up my legs to my thighs. I don't falter my movements or my stare on the man before me. By the time my panties are in view, the darkness in his eyes has turned molten with lust.

"Open your legs wide," he orders. Deft fingers

toy with his belt, the thick leather whooshing through the loops of material, and a shiver trickles down my spine, ice and fire, burning me but leaving me cold, needy for him.

Obeying Lycan, I offer myself to him like a sacrifice, and the man before me, tall and foreboding, falls to his knees between my thighs. His large hands spreading me, opening my core to his heated stare.

He doesn't say anything for a long while, his thumbs slowly circling my smooth skin, sending goose bumps skittering in the wake of his touch. I watch in awe as he leans in, running his nose along the material of my panties as he inhales my scent. Even I can smell my arousal. Nobody has ever done this to me, taken me in like I was a fragrance to be savored.

His mouth presses down on me, my mound lifting against him as my needy whimper expels from my lips. "Please, Lycan," I plead, and I'm once again not sure of what I want from him. I'm unsure of what I need, but the man worshipping me like a deity knows. His thumb tugs at my panties, and I'm finally bared to his watchful stare.

Eyes burn with lust as he looks at my neatly trimmed pussy, and his mouth crashes down on me before his tongue laps at my folds. The sensation has my hips undulating against his ministrations as he teases and taunts with his lips. He fucks into me

243

with his tongue, opening my body to him.

I try to move, to shift, but I can't. His hold on me keeps me steady. The mattress beneath me is soft, the material silky against my fevered skin. Lycan's gaze locks on mine, and the view of this strong, powerful man eating me like I am his final meal sends my mind to the abyss of pleasure as my head falls back and I cry out. My legs tremble on either side of his face as his stubble tickles my inner thighs.

"Look at me, little red," Lycan commands from his kneeling position, causing me to snap my gaze to his. "Good girl." Two words send pride through me, and I can't stop smiling down at him. "Are you ready to take my cock in this pretty little cunt?"

"Yes, please?" Another plea. Another poignant admission of just how much I do want him. "Please, Lycan."

"Good," he praises before rising to his feet. With his mouth wet from my arousal, he grips my hair, tugging me forward until my lips are on his. The taste of my pleasure coats my tongue as I dance it along his lower lip.

With a quick kiss, he releases me, and I watch as his slacks are shoved to the floor along with his boxer briefs. His cock, thick and angry, juts out toward me. A gasp tumbles from my mouth when he fists himself in one hand, causing the tip to weep with pleasure.

"Taste it," Lycan whispers, and I obey easily. No is fight left inside me because all I crave is him. My lips wrap around his shaft, the saltiness of his cum mingled with the taste of me has my body aching to be owned.

"Please fuck me," I beg shamelessly because there is no longer any room for being shy or playing innocent. Because around Lycan, I'm not. I'm his, and I want him to know that. The thought of running from him before our wedding has left my mind, and now all I can think of is him inside me.

He doesn't need me to ask him twice. Seconds later, he's hovering over me, my legs spread around his waist, and the wetness of his tip nudges my entrance. His gaze holds mine, waiting for the moment I'm filled, and I don't wait long.

His hips move as he thrusts inside my entrance, the thickness of him stretching me almost painfully, causing me to cry out as bliss fills my lungs, and electricity sparks my nerves. Every inch of me is alight with pure lust.

"Fuck," Lycan growls, lowering his forehead to my shoulder, his hands bunching the sheets beneath me as he grits his teeth. "You're so fucking tight, little red," he murmurs along the nakedness of my shoulder, the heat of his breath fanning along my skin. "My cock is going to be forever etched inside you."

"Yes," I hiss out my response as Lycan pulls out slowly, then slams back in. My back arches as euphoria slams into me like a tidal wave, sending me to the precipice. I'm on the edge, waiting to leap into the abyss. His movements are slow and controlled, but I dig my nails into his shoulder, dragging them down his back until I reach his hips. I grip them tight, pulling him deeper into me as I lift my ass from the mattress.

"Jesus fucking Christ, you're a bad fucking girl."

A giggle escapes me. Lycan's movements hasten. He pulls out and drives back in, his cock hitting so deep inside me it's almost painful. I crave more though, and when I arch once more, his one hand grips my throat so tight, I see stars. He doesn't choke me harshly, but as his fingers dig into either side of the slender column, I find pleasure, and my body awakens with newfound release as I soak his cock with my arousal.

"That's it," Lycan coos, still gripping my neck with a dangerous hold. His lips feather along my cheeks before he reaches my ear. "Come on my dick again while I choke the breath out of you." The command sends me over that cliff-edge, and I fly into the darkness as the bright lights behind my lids dance.

His cock thickens inside me. He opens me wider while I pulse around him. Lycan's hips slam me into the bed, fucking me with violent desire, and the bitter vows I promised him earlier are nothing more than a distant memory.

He doesn't relent as my orgasm shatters me like a splintered glass, leaving me in fragments on the soft comforter. His body owns me with every drive of his cock. The moment he finds his own pleasure, he growls into my mouth. "Give me your breath." I obey as he releases my neck, sending waves of ecstasy through every inch of my body. My lungs inhale passion and expel happiness as he swallows every lungful of air, and I can't stop the whimpers and mewls, but Lycan greedily breathes them in too.

LYCAN

Pacing the carpet of my office, I run my fingers through my hair, tugging at the strands. In the other hand, I have my mobile pressed against my ear. The silence that greets me is nothing new, but the breath that comes from the speaker is confirmation he's there.

"What the fuck do you want?" My voice is cold, filled with the rage I've built over the years, the same anger that has spurred me in my hatred of the man I was meant to love. The man I called brother. "I'm done playing games with you, Darius. There is nothing you can do to me that can make matters worse. You chose to leave. When you walked away, I was the one who kept the Shaw name going."

"Did you? Or were you just so fucking blind to

our father's bullshit that you didn't see the truth? He cheated on Mom," Darius tells me. It's the same story he's been spewing for years, but there was never any proof. We're both the blood of our father, and there were never any other women.

"Don't give me that shit." I grit my teeth so hard my jaw ticks painfully. I'm certain I'm about to crack my teeth with the rage fueling me as I stare out the window each time I face it.

"The Shaw secrets will soon be revealed, brother," he tells me. I glance at Isaac, who is meant to be tracing the call. Only a few more moments, and I'll have him. I wait. "Do you really think I'm that stupid, Lycan?"

"I don't know what you mean."

He chuckles, the sound just like our father's. "Your pretty bride will wear your blood." His threat has me stilling all movement. I know he knows about Scarlett. "Her name will be the hue of her wedding gown." Isaac signals five seconds, and my heart rate spikes.

"You're a fool." Those are the last words I spew at my brother before the line goes dead. My gaze locks on the man I'm praying will give me good news, but instead, he shakes his head.

In a fit of rage, I fling my phone against the wall, watching it shatter into tiny pieces before it lies on the soft carpet of my office. The team Kahn had tagging Darius fucked up, and now Isaac wasn't able to trace the call.

My brother is clever.

And I'm fucking fuming.

"Isaac, go to the office and let Kahn know we've fucked up once again. Tell him I want this sorted. I want the whole team, not just two fucking imbeciles on the case. Darius needs to be found, and he needs to be found right fucking now."

"Yes, of course, Mr. Shaw," Isaac says as he quickly packs his laptop and tracing device away. The moment he's gone, I crack the knuckles of both my hands to stay calm, but the thought of my brother evading me once more only seems to make me angrier.

I spin around, facing the two ex-soldiers who are standing in my office. "This is why I asked you to keep tabs on him. How the fuck does he keep disappearing?" My fist slams against the wooden top of my desk, the thud loud and resounding in the office space. Anger surges through me as my men stand before me, shaking in their fucking combat boots.

"Sir," one of them says. He's been with us for a few months, and Kahn swore he's good. They knew each other while serving, but I'm not impressed with the bullshit they've fed me. The excuse is that they had taken a wrong turn, and the car Darius was in sped off in another direction. It's amateur, and I'll be talking to Kahn about it. "We fucked up, I understand, but we do have a location. We know he hasn't left the vicinity—"

I pin him with a glare which shuts him up quickly. "And how would you fucking know that?"

"The second team that was tagging him has scoured the roads. They picked up the SUV he's been driving." My rage eases slightly. Having my brother close by is dangerous because we're both volatile around each other.

"Then go back out there and find the fucker!"

They don't respond. Their answer is feet shuffling quickly out my office door. When I glance at the exit, I notice a pretty redhead staring at me with wide eyes. Last night, I took her once, and the second time, I tried to be gentle, but with those nails scraping down my back, I fucked her hard, and I'm certain she's still feeling the aftereffects.

"Come here," I command, allowing the anger to slowly dissipate because the sight of my soon-to-be wife walking toward me barefoot and dressed only in my shirt makes my dick take notice, and my mind focuses on her instead of the fuck up of my men.

"You sound angry," Scarlett observes, her gaze raking over my creased shirt and my slacks. I quickly pulled on this morning when Kahn called. When she reaches me, her hands cup my face, her thumbs circling my stubbled jaw. I had no time to shave this morning because I was too wrapped up in her naked body.

"I am. I was."

She tips her head to the side, her pretty lashes fluttering along her cheeks as she whispers her question. "Why?"

"My brother has evaded the tail I put on him."

"What is it about you two?" she questions, genuine curiosity dancing in her eyes as she watches my reaction, which is more than a wince, perhaps a grimace at the idea of retelling the story about my brother.

"Go and get dressed. I want to take you to Heaven," I tell her, ignoring the question but rather craving to have her in my club, in my private room where I can dominate her until I've had my fill.

Her mouth pops open as if she's about to ask why, but I pin her with a look that says don't ask questions. She moves effortlessly from my office, and I quickly tap out a message to Kahn to ensure it's all set up for when we arrive. Tonight, my little red will learn more about her future husband and just how he enjoys his games.

SCARLETT

When we walk into the club, the breath is knocked from my lungs. The dark yet decadent interior is drenched in pure elegance. This is not what I expected when Lycan told me it's a club where people come to act out their most salacious fantasies.

Black and silver.

Deep tones of red and purple.

Low lights that only offer hints of depravity.

My first impression of Heaven is that its name suits the club. Everything drips with lush opulence. Even though I imagined it being more of a dungeon, a play on the idea of heaven, it's not. The black leather sofas that line the circumference of the club look soft and inviting. The bar is steel and wood, giving off the allure of luxury. Women and men fill the dimly lit space, some on their knees, others on stage. A scene playing out at the moment is of a woman bent over and bound, the man behind her spanking her with a wooden paddle.

I'm out of my depth.

So much so that I can't stop my face from heating in embarrassment. But Lycan's gentle touch at the base of my spine grounds me, and I turn to look up into those forest eyes.

"Are you scared?" he asks while leaning in close. The music is a low, sensual drone of classical music—a soundtrack of the desire sparking through the room. The air thick with lust, and all I can feel is Lycan against me.

"No." I glance at the scene again, the man now fingering the woman, her legs spread lewdly for the audience as she screams with pleasure as his four fingers slip between her slick, glistening folds. Desire burns through me at the thought of being open like that for Lycan, feeling his fingers dip into my body as he takes me higher.

"Is that something you'd want to try?" he whispers in my ear, sending more heat traveling down my spine all the way to the apex of my thighs.

"I… I don't know if I can."

He chuckles, the sound vibrating through him and into me. "Trust me, little red, you'll be able to take it. That isn't something I'd do on the first go, but we can most certainly get you wet enough to take my hand."

The thought causes my nipples to harden against the soft lace material of my bra. My heartbeat thrumming between my thighs, and my panties are already wet with arousal.

"And I'd love to hear you scream, just like she is right now," he warns over the echo of the submissive coming hard all over the stage. Her body wracked with pleasure as she shakes and trembles. Her face is etched in ecstasy. There's no doubt she is in heaven right now.

"I need a drink," I tell Lycan who only smiles as he leads me to the main area of the club. There are waitresses and waiters dressed in black and white who expertly hold trays of drinks as they swish amongst the guests. Lycan pulls me into his hold, my back to his front as I look around. His body is large, cocooning me against him.

"Lycan," a soft purr comes from our left, and I glance over my shoulder to find a beautiful woman with long blonde hair standing beside us. She's draped in a sheer, black dress with lace underwear visible through the material. Her nipples are pierced with silver barbells, and a blush warms me from face to chest. I instantly recognize her, the same woman from the gala at Bardot Manor.

"Nice to see you, Lori," Lycan greets her, but his hold on me tightens. Her blue eyes find my hazel ones. "This is my fiancée, Scarlett," he informs her, his voice controlled, calm, but there's a hint of satisfaction that elicits a smile from me.

"Nice to meet you." My words are sweet, but they're not entirely friendly or free of jealousy either. I didn't for one moment think Lycan didn't have a past, but the thought of this woman coming near him at any point has envy coursing through me.

She doesn't respond, merely nods before walking off, leaving me glaring at her exposed back. The dress she's wearing is barely there, and I wonder why she bothered.

"Who is that?" I don't look at Lycan as I ask this, because if I had to be honest with myself, I don't want to see any desire in his gaze for someone else. The possessiveness is new to me, catching me off guard.

I've never been *that* girl, who would lose her shit over another woman. If a guy is easily swayed, then I'm not the one for him. And vice versa. But right now, with the ring Lycan gave me weighing heavily on my finger, I feel his grip tighten.

"That is nobody," he tells me. "She was someone I spent a few scenes with, and she meant nothing to me, not like you do."

Turning in his arms, I stare into his gaze. "I

can't mean that much to you, not yet. I know we're getting married, and most times, it means you're in love with someone to walk down the aisle, but I don't want to fool myself into thinking I'm nothing more than a means to an end for you."

My acceptance of what Lycan and I are, came late last night. While I laid in bed alone, I thought about it. Knowing I will never have a marriage filled with love, I convinced myself I'd make myself happy. Perhaps if I had someone who could offer me what I lacked at home, with Lycan's agreement, of course, I could survive long enough to let Lycan have his vengeance.

It might sound stupid, but if I don't have another choice, I have to live with what life has thrown in my way. And that's something I learned from reading books. Where the heroine is forever looking out for herself, no matter what, I'll do the same.

"If you ever think you mean nothing to me, you're sorely mistaken," Lycan says, catching my attention, bringing it back to the here and now. "I may have signed a contract to marry you, but that doesn't mean you haven't slowly burrowed your way into my mind."

I note how he doesn't say, heart. He is convinced he cannot love. And even though my plan to make him fall for me has fallen by the wayside, his admission makes me think perhaps without trying,

I could still accomplish it.

"Then show me your world," I whisper, allowing my lips to feather along his, earning myself a growl of need. The wolf that Lycan keeps locked away within him is hungry, and he bares his teeth when I bite down on his full lower lip.

Lycan's animalistic hiss is nothing short of feral and wild. Even though we're amongst guests only a few feet away, I want nothing more than for him to touch me again. Memories spark in my mind like fireworks on the Fourth of July. He takes a step toward me, eating up the few inches that were there before, and his hand grips my hip possessively.

"Every fucking man in this room right now wants you," he murmurs under his breath, reminding me that we're not alone. That's the problem when I'm near Lycan. All I can think about is him; all I see is him. He looms over me, like a giant, and I feel small and fragile.

"No, they don't."

A chuckle reverberates through him. "You're far too fucking sweet and innocent. It's a shame that I'm going to have to mar that beauty," he tells me earnestly. "I'll show you my world. I'll train you to be the perfect little submissive, but there's one thing I want from you."

"Besides the bitter vows, I'm meant to spew at our wedding?" I challenge, causing a predatory smirk to curl his lips which causes my stomach to twirl with nervous energy.

"Let me tell you one thing, little red," Lycan whispers along my cheek in a trail to find my earlobe, which he grazes with his teeth. "When you say your vows in a couple of weeks, they'll not be bitter but filled with want and need. Because when I'm done with you, you'll beg to be my wife."

His fingers dig into my hip, painfully reminding me of who's in charge. He steps back quickly, as if he wasn't there to begin with. And then, he's leading me with gentle fingertips at the base of my spine as we move through the crowd.

I'm utterly speechless, and that's how Lycan guides me to the curved bar where two young, handsome men are working. One of them sees Lycan and straightens, offering a curt nod, but he doesn't greet him verbally.

"Simon," Lycan says in a tone that underlies dominance. "My fiancée will have a white wine. I'll have the usual."

"Yes, sir." He moves quickly, grabbing glasses and setting them before us. The display of obedience is something I'm convinced Lycan enjoys. This is what he wants from me, no debating, no snarky comments, only obedience.

Once our drinks are poured with a flourish and a hint of a smile, Lycan hands me mine and picks up his tumbler, which shimmers with amber liquid. "I'd like you to take it all in." His gaze flits behind me, and I can tell there's annoyance where moments ago there was happiness and comfortable satisfaction—as if he were home.

When I turn, I find the woman, Lori, staring at us. She's perfected the vamp look, and her sights are set on the man who's right beside me. Tall, leggy, and someone I would picture Lycan beside rather than me.

"Are you going to lie to me again?" I question, but I don't turn to face him. I can't see the denial on his face when he tells me she's nothing to him.

"Let's go," he answers, pulling me toward the back of the club, where we disappear down the hallway into a room decked in black. The reminder of his bedroom comes to mind, and I have a feeling this isn't just a random room that can be used. This is Lycan's bedroom of choice.

"Who is she?"

"The woman who took everything from me and left me with nothing. Now can you stop asking questions and take off your clothes," he orders through gritted teeth. His free hand tangles in his dark hair, while his other brings the drink to his full lips as he swallows back the double shot of whiskey.

This is not the way I thought this evening would go.

Obeying him without debate, I slink off the black dress, and I stand before him in matching black panties and a bra that pushes my breasts together, giving me the illusion of cleavage.

His hot stare takes me in from my heels, which are a dark red. His gaze trails me gently, and it feels like his hands are all over me.

The straps of my shoes hold my feet as if it were Shibari rope binding my body. He stops his perusal briefly when he reaches the tie at the ankle, which is a silver clasp. My long, lean legs are bare, leading to my panties that are a delicate lace material, hiding what I know he wants to see.

My flat stomach tingles when he eases his stare upward, and it stops on my breasts, which are encased in the same lace material as my pussy. My nipples peak, hardening against the fabric until he finds my eyes.

"I want so much to hurt you," he murmurs before setting the glass down. "I want to see you cry, make you scream." His words instill fear, but the flurry of wings in my stomach confirm that I want it.

"Is that what would give you pleasure, Master?" I question, using the word I only know from reading romance novels to affect men like Lycan Shaw.

His smile is pure satisfaction. He didn't expect me to say it, to gift him the title I've never before mentioned—his title of my owner. I step toward him slowly, and for a moment, I think he's going to get angry, but instead, he watches like a predator.

When I'm inches from him, I lower myself to my knees. The soft carpet under me is gentle against my skin, and I bow my head in a show of submission I know will turn him on. The thought has my pussy tingling, and I'm certain I'll soon be wet with need.

"Put your hands behind your back and look me in the eye." His order comes out gruff and husky. And once more, I obey easily. Lycan steps back, taking in my kneeling form before he walks over to a cabinet against the far wall.

A clinking of metal sends ice through my veins, but when he turns to regard me, I notice they're only cuffs. At least that won't hurt. When Lycan returns to me, he crouches behind me, binding my hands together.

He helps me to my feet, and soon, I'm bent over the edge of the mattress, my arms straining behind me. My arms are bound with cuffs that fit around my wrists and forearms, allowing my hands to rest on my lower back, giving him access to my butt.

Another click of something echoes in the room. Seconds later, I'm immobile because what I didn't realize is Lycan had a spreader bar, which has now locked my feet apart. I would be bare to him if he were to pull my panties down.

"Choose a safe word," Lycan says. "Something

you'll remember, something unique. If you at any point say it, I'll stop." He crouches down, so we're eye to eye, and I don't recognize the man before me. The wolf has taken over. He's no longer Lycan but a beast in need of feeding.

The word comes to me easily, and with a smile, I say, "Wolf."

The corner of his mouth quirks, and he nods. Leaving me to stare at nothing but the wall on the far side of the bed.

I watch from my viewpoint, which doesn't allow me to see much. He moves across the room, fiddling with something in the corner, and when it sparks to life, I hear a stereo. Music drifts from the corners of the room, a familiar tune.

Sofia Karlberg sings "Lonely Together", and my heart aches in my chest when I listen to the lyrics as Lycan picks up a thick leather flogger. Nervous energy trickles through me when he nears me, and for a moment, I'm scared.

"Don't be afraid," he tells me as if sensing my fear. "I'll take it easy." The agony in his voice makes my chest tighten, and tears spring to my eyes. I want to know what's hurting him, why he's doing this, but I don't ask.

When the first lashing of leather kisses my skin, a hiss escapes me. He doesn't stop; he continues, another and another. With my arms behind me, the tips of the flogger touch my back in small spurts.

Lycan lowers his attack to my ass, sending heated tingles to my pussy, causing mewls of pained pleasure to escape my lips. I screw my eyes shut in an attempt to focus on not coming, because surprisingly, I'm close to the edge.

"If you come, I'll hurt you. I promise you that, little red."

"Please, Sir," I plead, the words coming to me easily because I'm not sure I can hold off. He continues his assault down to my calves and back up to my ass before he drops the flogger, and suddenly, an ice-cold item slides along my skin. When it slithers under the material of my panties, I realize it's a blade.

A gasp escapes me when Lycan cuts my panties from my body. The material falls to the floor, and I'm open to him now. My wetness is evident as he grips my ass cheeks, opening my body to his gaze.

"So pretty when you're wet and needy." His voice is dark and gruff with desire. Suddenly, his hand comes down on my pussy, causing a cry of pain to stumble free from my lips. His fingers taunt and tease as he opens me before slapping me once more.

My legs shake, my body trembles, and my mumbling pleas for him to allow me to come are a symphony alongside the sad song playing in the background. Lycan continues with his alternating torture of slapping and fingering, my arousal soaking down my thighs.

"I think my little red needs my cock," Lycan says from somewhere behind me, but I'm too far gone to even respond to him. With two more swats on my ass, he drives into me with one long thrust, causing me to scream as pleasure wracks through my body, and I fall over the edge into darkness.

"Bad girl," he coos, but he likes it, it's a good thing because I'm not punished for being bad. Instead, he fucks me hard. His hips slamming me into the bed, his body looming over me as he hisses in my ear, "This time, I'll be nice," and I can hear the amusement in his tone when he says the word nice. "But next time you come without my permission, I'll make you cry."

With that, he grips my throat, pulling me back, so our bodies are flush. His mouth on my cheek, his warm breath sending more heat skittering through my veins.

His thick cock opens me, driving in so deep I'm left breathless with every thrust. Sweat drips from my skin as he takes me brutally. But I can't stop the pleasure from taking me higher and higher until I'm screaming something incoherent because all I feel is him.

I'm nothing more than a ragdoll for him to use,

and I'm not at all angry about it.

Lycan's free hand swats at the front of my pussy while his cock thickens inside me, and another orgasm breaks free from deep in my gut as he growls his release inside me. He stills behind me, still holding onto my throat while his other hand now gently massages my clit.

"My good girl," he coos finally before allowing me back to the mattress. He uncuffs me before unlocking the spreader bar. Once he drops the items to the floor, he pulls me into his arms, and we settle on the bed, Lycan's arms around me, holding me tightly against him, and I've never been happier.

My lashes flutter closed, and I realize I'm falling deeper with every moment I spend with him. He's opened my eyes to something more, and I don't think I could ever return to the girl I was before.

And that thought scares me as I fall into a dreamless sleep.

LYCAN

The sun hasn't even risen yet, and I'm planning something I'm not sure Scarlett will approve of, but my gut has been churning with worry for days, and this is the only way I know my plan will work.

When I spoke with Kahn, he told me I should go ahead with this, so we're about to do it. A knock at my office door has me glancing up to find the devil himself walking in. Kahn looks happy with himself as he settles in a chair opposite my desk.

"Priest is ready," he tells me.

"And Simon?"

He nods. "He's willing to be a second witness. We have everything. We just need a bride," he informs me.

"I need to talk to her. She's still asleep," I inform

him. "Give me some time. Tell him to be here at eight. I'll make sure Scarlett is ready."

"Are you sure this is the way to go about it?"

I know his concerns about the very public wedding on Saturday, but if Darius is going to attack, it's going to be there. I need her to have my name, my protection by then. "If something happens, get her to the convent. Stay with her. Don't let that fucker near her."

Even though I'm ready for my brother, I have to have a plan in place if all goes to shit. Knowing my life, it's most definitely going to go to shit the moment I'm standing at the end of the aisle as I wait for her to reach me.

Pushing to my feet, I head to the door with Kahn following. "I trust you," I tell him. "I know you'll make sure she's safe until I can get to her."

"She will be safe. I'll put my life on the line for her. The same goes for you." I know he's telling the truth because that's what this man has always done for me.

He leaves me as I walk down the hall to the bedroom where I left her earlier. Upon entering, I find my sweet bride sitting amongst the black silk sheets with her skin bare and beautiful.

"Good morning," I greet as I make my way toward her.

"Hi," she says. "Where were you?"

I lean in to press a kiss to her forehead. "I needed to do some business. I have something I need to talk to you about." When I settle on the mattress, I can read the fear in her expression.

"What's wrong?"

Sighing, I take her hand with the ring on her third finger in mine and meet her questioning stare. Better to rip the Band-Aid off quickly. "I want us to get married today."

"What? Why?"

"Our wedding on Saturday will go ahead, but I want you to have my name and protection before that day comes." I keep my gaze on hers. "I just want you to be safe if anything were to happen."

She watches me for a long while before saying, "You're worried about your brother." I nod, and she continues. "Do you think he'll do something at the wedding? I mean, there'll be guests, and your team will be there."

"I don't put anything past my brother." It's true. I don't trust him. And I most certainly wouldn't trust him not to hurt Scarlett, and I find fear choking me at the thought of something happening to her.

I look into those pretty eyes and find affection. Love. My lungs struggle to pull in air when I realize those emotions are reciprocated. All the fights, debates, and arguments have brought us both here.

It was about revenge.

It was about her father.

But right now, it's no longer about those things.

"This is us," I tell her. "Bitter vows aside," I tease with a grin. "I want you, little red. I crave and hunger for you constantly. You're mine, and you always will be. I just… I need you to know that before we walk down the aisle. And the only way I can do that is to say my vows today."

A small smile graces her pretty face. "Okay. Then we'll get married today."

Seeing Scarlett walk out of the bedroom in a bright red dress that hugs every curve of her frame has me coughing into my hand to keep the growl from escaping my lips. She looks like pure seduction, a beautiful vixen walking to her death as she takes my hand.

"Are you ready?" I ask before pressing a kiss to her knuckles.

"As ready as I'll ever be." She notices the men standing to the side waiting for us. Kahn, Simon, and the priest I had Kahn find last minute. I woke up this morning with the thought of marrying her today, and I needed to make it happen.

"Shall I start?" the priest asks, who I recall is named Arthur.

"Yes." I nod, taking both Scarlett's hands in mine.

With a nod, he begins. "We have gathered here today to lawfully bind Scarlett Bardot and Lycan Shaw in holy matrimony. Since they will be saying their own vows, I'll ask Scarlett to speak first."

My girl inhales a deep breath before smiling up at me. Her light shines through her expression, her eyes are shimmering with emotion, and I ache to steal every moment of this day and commit it to memory. I'm not sure what's going to happen tomorrow, but for today, I'm basking in happiness I never thought I would feel.

"For weeks, I was convinced when I finally said my vows they'd be filled with bitterness and rage," Scarlett says with a soft smile. "But I no longer find those emotions in my words." She holds my hands as if I were a lifeline. "This isn't how we were going to do this, but I, Scarlett Bardot, take you Lycan Shaw in happiness and sadness. I'll walk through heaven and hell beside you, as long as you're the one ruling over the kingdoms. Our path ahead may not be paved with ease, but I cannot wait to see what lies before us."

My chest tightens considerably, and I realize for the first time in my life, I'm falling. I've fallen. I've never expected to find happiness with someone, not with a woman who is filled with so much innocence and light.

But here she is.

"The darkness inside me has eased because of you," I tell her. "We may not be standing before hundreds of people, and you aren't wearing a pretty white dress, but even as we do this in my club, I know our future will be filled with happiness. I vow, bitter or not, to keep you, hold you, cherish you, and ensure you're forever smiling."

A tear escapes her lashes, trickling down her cheek, but I don't steal it because I love to see how those pretty eyes glisten with emotion just for me.

"I'm not the prince, I'm the wolf, but I'll forever keep you safe from the hunter who aims to steal you from me." I lean in, my lips brushing along her. "From today and forever more."

"I love you," Scarlett says suddenly, causing my heart to still in my chest for a second before thumping wildly against my ribs. "I didn't think it was possible." She smiles, shaking her head slowly. "But somehow, you've battered down my walls."

Cupping her face, I run my thumbs along the apples of her cheeks, and I can't stop the grin that cracks along my face. "I love you too, little red," I admit honestly. "I really do. Fuck the arrangement with your father. This" — I pull her closer — "this is real."

Scarlett giggles playfully, and she kisses me

as the priest sighs that we've completely fucked his ceremony. "I now pronounce you husband and wife," he says as I pull my wife into my arms. Even though our wedding will still go ahead for the guests, today is for us.

SCARLETT

My grandmother looks over at us, watching from afar, but peering in so closely she may as well be standing beside us. I've enjoyed my time in New York while learning more about Lycan's world, the dark and twisted cravings of a man whose beast lies in wait for when I kneel for him.

I didn't think I would.

But the wolf who appears when Lycan hungers for me is nothing like I've ever experienced. He's like a bomb waiting to explode, and I want nothing more than to be right beside the destruction he leaves in his wake.

Time has passed, making me more aware of how easily I've fallen into a life with him. Fallen in love with a man who bought me. It sounds like the makings of a romance novel. But it's my real life. And I couldn't be happier.

The buildings we've visited in the hopes of me finding one for my company have given me pause. When I was first taken to the Shaw mansion in Crimson Falls, I was convinced I would be free of him within the week. But now, I find myself more enthralled with him.

The wedding is fast approaching, and with more plans being confirmed—venue, food, guests— I'm no longer nervous. I don't necessarily want to walk down the aisle so soon, but I no longer hate the man who's currently speaking to Kahn while pacing the living room carpet.

We head back to Crimson Falls tomorrow to finalize the last details for the big day, but something has been bothering Lycan for a couple of days. And I have a feeling it's because of whatever Kahn is currently telling him.

And I'm sure it has something to do with his brother.

I approach my grandmother, wanting to talk to her without Lycan listening. By the time I reach her, she's finished her wine and asking for another. I'm not sure why she came when she doesn't seem happy about the engagement.

Even though this party was meant to celebrate our union, Lycan and I are aware of her animosity toward the upcoming nuptials.

"I thought you'd be happy," I say when I step beside my grandmother. I can't tell her I'm already married to him, so I play along as if nothing has changed since she last saw us.

She doesn't answer for a beat, but then says, "Nothing about a Shaw and Bardot together should bring about happiness."

"Is that because your heart was broken by a Shaw?" I challenge, because she knows that I know about her and Conall. Perhaps I shouldn't goad her, but I need to know about the curse that has been whispered about.

"The past needs to stay buried, but your man keeps dredging it up," she whispers, nudging her chin toward where Lycan is now talking to a couple of guests, his call ended, and I wonder what the outcome was.

"I don't understand what the problem is about learning something that happened to our families." I don't look at her this time. Instead, my focus is on the way Lycan's fake smile is plastered on as he watches us. He's not listening to what the man beside him is saying.

"There are some secrets that should never be brought to light. I made mistakes, I admit that, but when I walked away from my past, from Conall, I promised him to never allow our families to unite.

It's wrong."

This time, I spin on my heel to regard her. "What's wrong about it?"

Her gaze glints on mine. "Do you love him?" she asks, a challenge in her words.

Do I?

Yes. I do.

Am I attracted to him?

Do I lust after him?

Yes, and yes.

There's no doubt in my mind Lycan is my other half, a match I didn't expect. Love wasn't something I expected to feel, but it's there now, and I'm not letting it pass me by. I didn't expect him to say it, to tell me those three words, but he did. At least, he didn't seem anywhere near emotions that strong. But his heart is beating for me now, and I've got a grasp on it.

"If you don't love him, tell him. Stop this farce of a wedding," my grandmother says softly, but the urgency of her tone is clear. She doesn't want this wedding to go ahead.

I grin because I know what she's trying to do. Mom said she did this at their wedding as well. When my mother and father were to wed, Gran thought she could stop it, or control it. Instead of answering, I challenge, "And if I don't?"

This time she looks directly at me, her gaze lingering on my face as if she's taking in every inch of me to memory. "Nothing good will come of it." She swallows back her drink before making her way for the door, and I watch as my grandmother disappears without looking back.

A cold shiver races down my spine.

Awareness that her warning will come with dire consequences.

The dress is stunning, just like I knew it would be. I wanted today to be perfect. Over the weeks of getting to know Lycan, seeing his pain about how his father died and how his brother didn't believe a word of what had happened, I understand why he is so closed off.

But he did open up to me.

He gave me parts of himself I'm certain not many people were privy to. And it means a lot to me to have moved forward, to have overcome what I believed about him before. He's not a monster at all. Perhaps a beast, yes, but he's all man.

I didn't think I could ever find it in myself to love him like I should—as a husband. But I do. And I would like to try to find my path alongside him, to walk forward today down the aisle and know that my future is safe. To know the man I'm saying "I do" to is someone capable of love. Deep down, I know Lycan is.

There's no longer any doubt in my mind.

The sleek, white dress hugs my curves, and the lace train lays behind me along the carpet. As the two maids Lycan hired to dress me fix the tiara to my head along with the veil, I glance at myself in the mirror, taking in the elegance.

My bedroom door swoops open, and Aelin rushes in. "Oh my god," she gushes when she sees me. "You look incredible." Her voice bounces off the walls as she stops in front of me, her hands on my shoulders as she holds me at arm's length.

"I'm so glad you're here," I tell her honestly. When I asked Lycan if she could be my maid of honor, he agreed. When his humanity shines through the cold exterior, I can't help but smile because as much as he tries to hide it, I know he cares deeply for me.

"I cannot believe you're getting married."

Once the women are done with my hair, they leave us, and I settle onto the stool provided, so I don't crease my dress. Even though I'm not yet in my heels, I need to sit because my knees are shaking. I don't want to admit how nervous I am, so I paste on a smile and look at my one and only friend.

"Trust me, if you had asked me a month ago if I would be here, getting ready to walk down the aisle,

I would've told you you're crazy," I admit easily.

"This man must be all that because the Scarlett I know would never allow a man to dictate anything about her life," she says. "Or is it *because* he has a big dick?" Her teasing has me laughing, and for a moment, I enjoy the lighthearted banter between us. It's been so long since I've seen her, going from talking to someone every day to not seeing them for weeks is strange.

"I am not talking about his dick," I throw back, knowing my best friend will be asking more about Lycan, as well as any dirty details about our sex life. Aelin was more provocative than I was, even when we came of age, she would go out to parties, meet boys when I would be the wallflower. I couldn't find the courage to tell her about my tastes. Not the ones I hid in the dark for so long.

Those same fantasies Lycan brought to life.

I should've spoken to her more. Over the past few weeks of me being here, I should have reached out. Even though Lycan didn't forbid me from calling, I didn't. Perhaps it was because I couldn't really explain my situation. My father put me here, he forced my hand without my permission, and as much as I wanted to hate him, I'm thankful he showed me his true colors.

"Are you okay?" Aelin asks then, her hands holding mine, pulling them close as she regards me with earnest curiosity.

"Yes, I am." It's the truth. If she had asked me when I first arrived here, I would've said no. But I truly am okay. "It's been eye-opening."

"Oh, I'm sure it has." She wiggles her eyebrows, amusement brightening her face as she takes me in. I can feel the heat on my cheeks. But she doesn't press me for more information. Thankfully. "So, where's my dress?"

"Over in the garment bag hanging on the back of the door," I tell her, pointing to where she came in. Now that we're shut in, she can see the item. Aelin rushes to it, unzipping it quickly to find the dark crimson dress that reminds me of a rich, red wine.

I didn't want pinks or blues, or any pastel color, and the red just fit so perfectly with what I had envisioned when we decided to have the wedding at the house. With vast gardens, and the beautiful scenery that overlooks the woods, I envisioned a fairytale wedding.

"This is epic," Aelin remarks as she strips down to her underwear and slowly slides the satin over her frame. It fits perfectly, like I knew it would. And when the straps are draped over her shoulders, I can't help but grin.

"I knew you'd pull that off," I tell her quickly as I push to my feet and rush to her side. Her long, blonde hair hangs to the middle of her back in waves of silk. "This is perfect. I wanted something different."

"I must say, the color scheme is totally you," she tells me with a giggle. "But I love it. I just want this day to be perfect for you." Once again, she takes my hands in hers, and emotion pricks at my eyes. I was so convinced I would walk away from Lycan before I got to this day. I wanted to escape, but right now, all I want to do is walk down the aisle.

"It's perfect because you're here, and you get to share it with me," I tell her honestly. "But don't make me cry. They spent hours on my makeup," I tease, offering a smile as I try to keep the tears at bay.

"Well, let's not keep your future husband waiting."

"I'll be there in a moment." I watch her go after a quick hug. Once alone, I take a few deep breaths before I pick up my phone. There's one person I need to talk to before I do this, one person I need to ask one simple question before I say, "I do."

DARIUS

For years I've waited. Needed proof before I walked into my brother's home and told him the truth about our family. About our father. As much as I loved him, I knew he was bad news. I learned a long time ago the Shaw name wasn't all it was cracked up to be. There were things hidden in closets, secrets, things he didn't want to have come to light.

And even then, I knew I couldn't be the man my father wanted. Yes, he was good to us as kids, but the older we got, the more I learned about who he truly was. Our mother, a woman who had loved him unconditionally, wasn't only just a pawn in his game, but she was a stand-in for the person he truly loved.

Lycan may have believed otherwise, and I

allowed him to, but now as he takes a wife, he needs to learn the truth about the pretty redhead he'll share a bed with. Today is the wedding, and it amuses me that I've chosen a suit and tie to wear to the event. The black jacket hugs my rather large frame, with slacks that just fit.

A white button-up is not my choice of clothing, but for my brother, I'll do it. I need to blend into the crowd until I have my opportunity to stand and tell him the truth. I didn't want to do it this way, but I don't have a choice.

When I called my mother, I asked her to do it, to admit the shitshow she'd brought upon our family, but she refused. Which only leaves me with one option. I don't feel bad about it. The anger, the rage I've lived with knowing I was cast aside because I wasn't willing to fall into line, has made me hate everyone.

Lycan.

Scarlett.

Even Grace.

Picking up my weapon of choice, I screw on the silencer and smile down at the black metal that lies heavily in my hand. I found a family, and they gave me a gift I could never thank them enough for. Knowing I'm a killer is one thing but realizing the next person I'm about to murder in cold blood is my brother, well, that's another thing altogether.

Being a biker outlaw, I've seen my fair share of dead bodies. It doesn't faze me anymore. I doubt it ever will again. Lycan doesn't realize the first kill I ever made wasn't our father. He may believe it, and when I tried to tell him the truth, he didn't want to listen, so it's time I righted the wrongs of my brother and I.

Making sure my gun is strapped to my shoulder holster, I shrug on the jacket and pick up my keys. My mobile phone is off. My wallet in my pocket, I head out to the car. It's only a few blocks away, but I will need to get away from the mansion as quickly as possible.

In the driver's seat, I start the engine and pull out onto the road toward the house. When I reach the spot I marked out days ago, I come to a stop and sit watching the guests make their way inside.

Excitement churns in my gut, a reminder that soon I'll be reunited with the memories, the truth, and the admission that comes with what I'm about to say. A limo pulls up, and as the back door opens, *she* gets out. Her black dress is evidence that she's not happy about the union.

I knew she wouldn't be. And she would've made it known.

I exit my own car and make my way around the house. I blend in as I move through the crowd of guests and up the stairs. Lycan would be in his office by now, talking to Kahn about security.

Nobody would seek me out.

Nobody would even bother asking who I am.

There are so many strangers here today. I'm just one of the many faces. I've ensured my hair has been cropped short from the ponytail I usually sport. My beard has been shaved, and my hazel eyes are now dark brown from the contacts. I look nothing like Darius Shaw.

I hear them usher the guests to the garden, but I quickly race up the steps onto the landing and take a right toward her room—my brother's fiancée. The door opens, and out comes her best friend, Aelin.

I've had to learn all about the pretty blonde when I was doing my research. The moment she sees me, her eyes widen. "Who are you?"

"Who are you?" I throw back, offering her a smirk which seems to have the effect I need.

She grins. "I'm the bride's best friend, Aelin." She holds out a dainty hand, which I accept, bringing her knuckles to my lips and pressing a kiss to the smooth skin.

"Well, it's lovely to meet you," I tell her before releasing her. I keep her stare, holding her hostage with a mere glance. "I trust you'll enjoy the show." I straighten and leave her staring at my back as I step into the bathroom not far from Scarlett's bedroom.

I wait inside listening to the music change,

and when they play the bridal march, I step out of the bathroom and find Scarlett in the hallway. The darkness enveloping her from the dim light of the interior of the house.

She spins on her heel when she hears the door click, and her gaze widens when she takes me in. I can see the wheels spinning in her head. She's trying to place me, but she won't recognize me. I know she won't.

"Scarlett," I greet with a bow. "It's so lovely to see you."

Confusion creases her brows. "I'm sorry. I don't think we've met."

Nodding, I gift her a lie. "I'm one of Lycan's acquaintances. An old friend, so to speak." For a moment, I'm almost certain she's going to scream, but I would happily shut her up with a hand to her throat, but when she nods, I ease the tension in my shoulders.

"It would be an honor to escort the bride to the aisle," I tell her with a charming grin plastered on my face. I offer her my elbow, and she slowly but gratefully accepts with a smile.

"Thank you. I can't find anyone," she tells me with a soft, gentle tone that makes the blood in my veins boil with anger.

I shouldn't hate her.

It's not her fault.

We walk out onto the landing and take the steps down to the foyer. Turning left, I lead her toward the patio doors. The moment we step out onto the soft grass, I glance up and grin at Lycan, who looks like he's ready to kill.

Walking down the aisle is surreal as I hold onto Scarlett's hand. The gun in my shoulder holster feeling heavier with every step. We're almost at the end of our march when I reach into my jacket, flashing the metal at my brother, whose eyes widen.

A gasp of guests from behind me doesn't deter me. That's when I hear feet shuffling and a few of the women screaming. I don't turn. My focus is laser sharp. He puts his body between the gun and Scarlett, but he doesn't need to worry. I won't hurt her.

When I first heard he'd signed the agreement for her hand, I thought it was a lie. I figured he was doing it merely for revenge. But now I see he does have feelings for her because he steps forward, taking her hand in his. He tugs her toward him, and he leans in. The whisper he gifts her with causes her to flick her gaze toward me, which is evidence that he's just told her who I am.

He pushes Scarlett behind him. "Hello, brother," I mutter. "Call your pack of hounds off."

He offers a nod, and I hear the clicking of weapons from behind me. "What are you doing here?"

"I came to give you the truth." I hand him the paper I had folded up in my pocket for the past two weeks. The proof that I'm not my mother's son. I'm not Lycan's full-blood brother.

He takes the page, and Scarlett tries to read from over his shoulder. She's a tiny thing. Fragile. Something I can break only to get revenge on the man before me.

"This is fucking ridiculous," he spits, throwing the proof to the floor like I knew he would. He thought I was lying all these years. When I glance to the left, I find my mother staring at me in horror. All the guests have gone. It's only her. She waited for me to show my face. She didn't think I would.

"Hello, Mother." I smile at her, causing Scarlett to gasp in shock. And that's when I pull the gun from my holster and aim it at my brother. "I'm here to do the job you asked me to do."

Grace pushes to her feet elegantly. That's one thing about her — she always had an air of grace about her. I suppose her name suits her.

"Put the gun down," she says, but I smile, ignoring her. "This is not needed."

I turn back to Lycan. "This is what she asked for," I tell him, nudging my head to the side. "With you gone, Grace will gain everything. Why do you

289

think she didn't want you marrying Scarlett?"

"What?" This comes from the pretty redhead. Her confusion is clear as she steps forward, but Lycan's arm comes out, blocking her from being in my line of fire. "Is this true, Gran?"

"I had Darius when I was young and stupid. I thought I was in love with Conall. It was a stupid fairy tale that could never work."

Scarlett's mouth pops open in shock and anger. "I... But how?"

"Family time is over," I say, tired of the revelations. I came here with one job in mind, and I'm going to finish it. Grace promised me what is due to me, and I'm here to collect. "Grace, say goodbye to your granddaughter."

Lycan grips Scarlett, his gaze locked on mine as I cock the gun and take aim. The last word he utters to her is, "Go." And that's when I pull the trigger and hit him right in the chest.

"Lycan," Scarlett yells.

"I said fucking go!" His voice booms as he drops to his knees, and Scarlett moves, but she doesn't know the woods like I do.

She runs, and I smile. She knows I will follow. I will always follow her, even if it means I will be walking into the middle of a blood bath.

A war of my own making.

But what Scarlett doesn't know is that Lycan made sure she was bait for the hunter.

THE END... *for now*

Sneak Peek

Want the first chapter of Bitter Truths?
Keep reading!

DARIUS

Revenge is a dish best served with a side of vengeance.

I spent my life in the shadows, wanting to hide from the truth that I was nothing more than a product of my father's indiscretions. And even in the darkness, I knew the truth—nothing can mend what my father had broken.

Now I'm here, waiting, racing through the woods after a pretty little girl I learned is my niece. Her grandmother, my biological mother, had me when she was young and abandoned me. She left me with my father, then went off and married someone else. Anger surges as I recall the day she told me her story. When I asked for proof, she gave me the test results.

Darkness shrouds my actions as I near her running form, her white dress torn and dirty from her escape, but I'm almost there. I'm so close I can smell her fear as it emanates from her supple skin. I can hear her short breaths, and I can't stop my cock from jolting. Perhaps I shouldn't think about her sweetness in that way, maybe I'm broken, but seeing her run from me makes me hungry to have a taste.

Just a bite.

It couldn't hurt.

The woods are dense, but through the dark brown of the trunks, I focus on the white, the slight frame of the beauty that's running for her life. But what she doesn't know is I'm a hunter, one that can so easily capture her, but the chase is a part of who I am. It runs through my veins. Shaw blood burns hot when we're chasing our prey. Even Lycan knows this, and perhaps that's why he told her to run. He knew I'd enjoy this. He must've.

The last thing she heard was my brother shouting for her to run from me. And now, as I howl out into the darkness, I inhale her fear along with that sweet nectar of her perfume.

When she reaches the breach in the trees, a scream catapults from her lips when she realizes my family is waiting. The bikers who took me in as a young rebel are there, their arms wrap around her, and the moment she's bound, I stop behind her, knowing my breath is hot in her ear.

"Your wolf is dead," I tell her while fisting my hands at my sides. I want to hurt her, but that will come. And when it does, she'll wish she was dead. A sob of pure agony tumbles free from her mouth, and I can't help but smile.

Slade throws her into his truck, which had been waiting as I chased her through the woods. The SUV I hired is still parked near the house where Lycan's men will find it. I made sure of that. When they do, they'll see exactly what I want my brother to find.

I shot him. Twice.

Leaving him for dead was part of my plan, but a part of me wonders if he'll ever survive the wounds I inflicted. And I wonder if he'll get the gift which I left for him before he takes his last breath.

Bear pulls up beside me on his bike. The truck behind us keeps a safe distance, but I can practically feel Scarlett's rage from the backseat. I didn't plan on taking her. I wanted her dead, along with my brother, but stealing her is definitely a bonus.

Call it collateral. Grace will never want her granddaughter hurt, which means she'll ensure I don't take my anger out on the girl. Without my emotions, I can easily make Scarlett bleed for being born, but I'll keep her alive to ensure I get my money.

Hatred is the only thing I feel. Guilt no longer rules my life. When Grace told me what had happened in the past, she gave no inkling that I was even loved, so why should I care about her, or her little granddaughter?

I thought for a moment that Lycan would see the truth, that he'd finally stand beside me, but the moment affection flashed in his eyes for the girl, I knew I had lost him for good.

I waited, craved even, just to see my brother again, the boy I grew up with. But he was long gone.

For years we'd been at war, and now that war has ended by my hand. I focus on the road ahead, which will soon be riddled with teams of men who will seek vengeance for Lycan. But I'll be long gone.

My brother tracked me for years, but never caught me. I had to walk into his home for him to finally see me, but even then, I was in control. As always.

We head out onto the highway which will take us far from Crimson Falls, and with every mile I put between me and that shit hole, I feel the tension in my muscles ease.

Time and again I've wanted Lycan to see the truth behind all those old books and open those brick walls he loves to hide behind. I wanted him to realize things aren't always as they seem. I loved Crimson Falls once. I didn't want to leave. However, my home, everything I knew, was a lie.

When we reach the compound five hours

later, it's dark, but I'm eager to see her, talk to her. Swinging my leg over my bike, I turn to see Bear and Slade pulling the little minx out of the backseat. Her screaming and kicking are no match for the two burly men.

Bear grips her around the middle, lifting her as if she weighs nothing.

"Take her to the basement," I instruct him. "It's time for us to have a little family meeting."

He nods, moving to the back of the house where we have a shed with a basement. This is where we take the assholes who try to fuck with us. And it's where I interrogate them, ensuring they spill the beans about everything and everyone.

The staircase is gritty under my boots. The suit I'm still wearing doesn't fit in with the dirty room I enter. "There's my little niece," I grin as I near her. Bear has her bound to a chair, blood dripping from her mouth. "What happened?"

"Bit down on my fucking hand," he growls, showing me the teeth marks Scarlett left on the flesh between his thumb and forefinger.

I can't help but chuckle. "Feisty little thing. Aren't you?" I question, looking into eyes that remind me of her mother's. So many secrets, so little time.

"Fuck you!" Fire blazes in her glare, and I can't help but remind myself that she's not her mother.

She's definitely not Marinda, the woman I fucked hard against their kitchen counter while Horatio was sitting in Heaven with young women on his lap. But Scarlett doesn't know that. She reminds me so much of her mother, beautiful, filled with anger, and yet I can't stop my dick from throbbing behind my zipper.

"Such a filthy mouth," I observe. "Is that why Lycan was so enraptured by you?" Arching my brow, I don't wait for her to answer before I pull out my phone. I quickly find what I'm looking for and hit dial, tapping the speaker icon so Scarlett can hear.

"Hello?"

"Dad! Help me!" She screeches at the top of her lungs Even though hearing her beg should ensure the need for revenge is satiated, it's only anger that seems to surge through me and I backhand her across her face so hard, the chair topples over, taking Scarlett to the ground with it.

"What the fuck? Scarlett, is that you? What's happening?" The panicked tone of Horatio Bardot is like music to my ears.

"So many questions, Horatio," I finally respond after a moment. "I think your little girl needs a daddy," I tell him, my smirk curling as the pretty redhead glares up at me from the floor. Bear moves to pick her up, but I raise a hand to stop him.

"If you hurt my—"

"Do you care?" I challenge, cutting him off. "Because weren't you the one who signed her life over to Lycan Shaw?"

His response is guilty silence.

Tears glimmer in his daughter's eyes. Horatio doesn't know who I am. His mother never told him about his half-brother. But now isn't the time for a family reunion.

"What do you want?" The resignation in his tone makes me smile. First this bastard, and then his mother. I'll make sure they both pay for what they did to me, to my father, and to Lycan. As much as I hate my brother, he is blood.

"Fifty million in an account which cannot be traced. I'll send you the details." My gaze fixes on Scarlett. "I don't need any negotiations on this. It's the money for your daughter. Or will you sell her out again?" I hang up before the asshole can answer me or question why I'm doing this.

"Cut," a voice calls from behind me, calling me by my club name, which causes me to turn. "Ambulance arrived at the Shaw mansion, Lycan is in ICU, doesn't look good." Kai, our enforcer looks at me before his gaze lands on Scarlett. The flicker of desire in his eyes dance like a flame as he takes her in. The torn dress, which is gritty with dirt, her face has a couple of scratches along with my large handprint, the blood caked on her mouth, and the way her eyes flash with pure venom makes her every fucker's wet dream.

"Good. Keep me updated."

He nods but doesn't leave immediately. "If you need a hand…" He allows the sentence to hang heavy with promise. There is no doubt in my mind that every man who's sitting in the clubhouse would love to be left alone with Scarlett. And I doubt she'd survive.

"Leave," I order, keeping my tone level. I don't need them to know she's something to me. All they know is that she's collateral.

I don't trust people with information they don't need. This job has been in the making for years. And now that it's finally here, I can't have anyone fucking it up. I glance at Bear, who's awaiting his orders. The man is an animal, but he's tame compared to Kai.

"I've got it from here," I grit, needing to be alone with her for a moment.

"Sure, boss. Let me know if you need me down here." He glances once more at Scarlett before leaving us. The heavy thud of his steps echoes as he reaches the first floor and shuts the door behind him.

Once we're alone, I turn to her. "Would you like to sit up?"

"Fuck you!" She spits blood and saliva on the floor, which will only mix with the rest of the crimson from our evenings down here questioning criminals.

"You know, we can do this the hard way," I taunt. "I quite like it like that. I'm sure my brother trained you for the darkness that comes with a good hard beating."

Shock paints her pretty face like a mask as she regards me. I may not be able to fuck her violently, but I can make her scream. And I'm certain it would be a beautiful symphony to listen to.

"Why are you doing this?" Her plea is quieter than her curse. Tears trickle down her face, falling to the floor where her head is leaning on the cold concrete.

Tipping my head to the side, I regard her for a long while, contemplating if I should admit my pain to her. "Do you know what it's like to be sent away by your own parents?"

Scarlett's gaze lingers on my face before she nods. "Yes, yes, I happen to know what that's like. From the outside, my life might seem perfect. It might look like I have everything, but my father sold me to Lycan. He signed my life away."

"Did he? I mean, you didn't seem all too bothered to walk down the aisle to marry my brother." Rage simmers through me. Her words only seem to turn up the heat on my already volatile emotions. Perhaps that's why Lycan was so taken with her. She does something to a man. Her sweet innocence mingled with the seductiveness of a vixen.

"No, I wanted to marry him because I learned to love him," she spits out, a sneer curling her pretty face, and I want nothing more than to grip her by the neck and haul her up to my level where we're eye to eye. I want to see the fear in her eyes, not the goddamned fire. Because that shit makes me hard as fuck.

"And you think he loves you too?" I challenge. I've known my brother all my life. He isn't capable of love. Even when she left him all those years ago, I knew he didn't love Yasmine. She was nothing more than a slave he could find pleasure with. She enjoyed the darkness he exuded.

"Yes." Comes Scarlett's response. It's a mere whisper. And if it weren't so quiet down here, I wouldn't have heard it. "You killed him."

"Not yet," I answer quickly. It seems the shots weren't fatal. There's always time to right my wrongs. "But I'm sure when I see him again, I'll finish the job." Shrugging, I turn to grab a chair and drag it along the cold concrete, making sure that the noise is loud enough to cause Scarlett pain.

"Why do you hate him so much? Why do you hate me?"

I settle in my seat while considering her questions. When people are in danger, or when they're hurting, that's the question they always throw out. Why?

I ponder my response for a while, wondering if I should tell her more about myself. If I should offer her honesty. "I wanted nothing more than a family to care for, but what I got instead was shame for being who and what I was."

She shifts, tilting her head so she can truly look at me. But it's when she finally speaks, do I realize she's really concerned. "I don't understand."

It's not a plastered-on worry that's creasing her brows. She truly has no clue what her family is like.

Add Bitter Truths to your TBR NOW!

One Click on Amazon!
US: https://amzn.to/3cv9csU
UK: https://amzn.to/31oU6yL
AU: https://amzn.to/3u0mO51

CA: https://amzn.to/3lZsGIX

THANK YOU!

I'm so excited to have Scarlett and Lycan out in the world! I have to thank a few special ladies, Allyson and Sara for BETA reading this duet, and to Ashlee, without your amazing graphics, this book wouldn't come alive.

Thank you to my editor for working on this. And a massive thank you to Illuminate Author Services for proofing!

To the team at Greys Promo, you ladies ROCK! Thank you so much for everything you did to keep me in line and on deadline.

To my ADULT, Caroline for putting up with my bullshit. And for ensuring I'm on time for everything I would be late to if it weren't for you.

To my BEAUTY, Carolina, for helping me with the group, and for being so sweet when I forget everything I'm meant to do.

The Street Team, you ladies work your ass off to get my name out there, thank you. From the bottom of my little black heart, THANK YOU!

My Deviants!! I love my group, and you ladies make it so amazing to pop in every day when I need an escape from the world. Thank you!!

To my fellow authors who are there with advice, support, and just a general pick me up. Thank you. It means more to me than you know. Thank you for sharing my work with your readers, and giving me a friendship that is second to none.

To the bloggers, you ladies read, read, read, support, post, review, and you do it with a smile. Thank you!! We wouldn't be here if it weren't for you, so keep what you're doing, we appreciate you! #AllBlogsMatter!

Lastly, to the readers, thank YOU! It's because of you I'm able to put out book after book. Giving you what you ask for, and hopefully making you excited about the next book. Thank you for your reviews, keeping them SPOILER FREE ;) But most of all, thank you for buying our books. For your support, love, and encouragement.

Mad love, D x

STALK ME!

My exclusive reader group gets news on all up and coming releases, sales, and a chance at early ARC copy giveaways! Join us, we don't bite… hard ;)

Dani's Deviants
www.facebook.com/groups/danisdeviants/

Or sign up for my newsletter and get an exclusive novella not available for purchase anywhere!

Sign Up Now!
https://bit.ly/DaniVIPs

BookBub: http://bit.ly/DaniBookBub
Facebook: http://bit.ly/DaniFBPage
Instagram: http://bit.ly/DaniIG
Goodreads: http://bit.ly/DaniGoodreads
Amazon: http://bit.ly/DaniAmazon
TikTok: http://bit.ly/Dani-TT

OTHER BOOKS

Stand Alones
Choosing the Hart
Love Beyond Words
Cuffed
Fragile Innocence
Perfectly Flawed
Black Light: Obsessed
Among Ash and Ember
Cursed in Love (collaboration with Cora Kenborn)
Beautifully Brutal (Soldati di Sangue)
How the Mind Breaks
The Devil's Plaything
While She Sleeps (Dirty Heroes Collection)
It's Never Easy (Lady Boss Press)
Only One Night (Lady Boss Press)
Deviant (Black Mountain Academy)

Traction (Driven World)
Brazen Bachelor (Cocky Hero World)
Delicate Surrender

Taboo Novellas
Sunshine and the Stalker (collaboration with K Webster)
His Temptation
Austin's Christmas Shortcake
Crime and Punishment (Newsletter Exclusive)
Tempting Grayson

Crimson Falls Duet
Bitter Vows (Book #1)
Bitter Truths (Book #2)

Gilded Sovereign Series
Cruel War (Book #1)
Volatile Love (Book #2)

Sins of Seven Series
Kneel (Book #1)
Obey (Book #2)
Indulge (Book #3)
Ruthless (Book #4)
Bound (Book #5)
Envy (Book #6)

Vice (Book #7)

The Taken Series
Stolen
Severed

Four Fathers Series
Kingston

Four Sons Series
Brock

Carina Press Novellas
Pierced Ink
Madd Ink

Broken Series
Broken by Desire
Shattered by Love

The Backstage Series
Callum
Liam
Ryan

Forbidden Series
From the Ashes - A Prequel

ABOUT DANI

Dani is a *USA Today* Bestselling Author of seductive and deviant romance.

Her books range from the dark to emotional, but every hero is alpha, and each heroine is strong-willed, bringing the men down to their knees.

She now lives in the UK, after moving from Cape Town, with her better half who does all the cooking while she writes all the words.

When she's not writing, she can be found binge-watching the latest TV series, or working on graphic design. She has a healthy addiction to reading, tattoos, coffee, and ice cream.

www.danirene.com
info@danirene.com